Curmudgeon

(Book One: The Terraced House Diaries)

Samantha Henthorn ©2018

This is a work of fiction. Names, characters, business, events and incidents are the products of the author's imagination. Any resemblance to actual persons, living or dead, or actual events is purely coincidental.

This book is dedicated to the Whitefield Massive.

Chapter 1: August Apologies

On the day this all started, the sky was full of August apologies for a summer undelivered. The jubilant bounty of July had almost disappeared half-eaten by gangs of gastropods. Despite the rain, pastel-shaded summer clothes continued to be rotated in wardrobes across the North West of England (resulting in damp trouser ankles).

Most houses do not feel the need to complain; their heating comes on, and then goes off again. Doors open and close, foot traffic of fairy elephants wear down the floorboards, carpets and staircases. But then, most houses do not have to suffer the anguish of ruin, the suffering of internal clowns dragging them down. I was once known around these parts as a *'desirable residence'* folk aspired to habituate here. Why! Even Mr and Mrs Payne were of the well-to-do set in their day. Although I must admit, the sun did not shine brightly enough on Number One Curmudgeon Avenue for my cracks to be noted, assessed and remedied. Overall maintenance of my structure had been somewhat neglected in Mr and Mrs Payne's twilight years. Yet, my four storeys of Georgian revival architecture remained fit for purpose. Wind delivered wet rubbish and leaves in my corners. Frost cracked, creating unwanted crevices, which even a renovation facelift failed to repair.

Yes, I am a snob; and what of it? If I had a nose, I'd be looking down it right now, it is the only way I can protect myself against the intertwined lives of my new residents. When I was empty, I dreamt of perfect house guests. I personally would have liked nothing better than to be sold on to a grateful and charming family employed in middle management with high performing children. I'm a stone's throw from Whitefield tram station and a minuscule commute to Manchester... Ah! Such is life...

If I may, what follows is the tragedy of how poor Mr and Mrs Payne met their end. Resulting in what I have to put up with now - the story of how Harold, Edith and Edna ended up living together under my roof.

If I have to contend with this bunch of nincompoops, then so should you...

Chapter 2: Deirdre

'Whitefield, three six double three' Edna Payne pronounced into the phone. 'Yeeees, I see. Riiiiight, my goodness, I see. Yeeees.' Edna wound the telephone cord around her forefinger, a habit from the days of land-line telephones. 'I see' she continued followed with more 'I see and my goodness's.' Her younger sister Edith sat directly opposite her and listened in on the conversation. Edna did have the most inconsiderate habit of making and receiving telephone calls while she had company. But this call was different...

Poor cow, Deirdre, the elephant. She was meant to be on her way to Knowsley Safari Park to meet her new elephant boyfriend (the one from Chester Zoo did not work out, but the less said about that, the better). The dodgy lorry driver had taken a wrong turning, gone too far and turned back on himself. Deirdre and the driver were now lost, and this had never happened before to this poor cow...

Myth dictates that these generously proportioned mammals are frightened of mice. Not so in the case of Deirdre. Born into a circus in the 1980s she survived the journey to the UK from her cold country. Deirdre did not suffer fools gladly. Scared of mice? Pah! Those creatures are not important enough for Deirdre to fear!

Why then, had this dodgy lorry driver with his counterfeit driving licence and poor sense of direction been entrusted with the task of conveying this majestical creature to her new home? The haulage company undercut and outbid all their competitors, of course! Not impressed with the only available elephant mover, Deirdre had started to sniff a musty smell radiating from his body. It intruded like an unexpected visitor up her trunk. So disgusted was Deirdre that she broke loose from her harness and attempted to make a dash for clean air. The driver slammed on his brakes, lost control, and plunged his wheels of doom into oblivion until their journey terminated; quite dramatically in one of Morecambe Bay's static caravan parks. The lorry stampeded through rows of tin boxes until wholly and finally, Mr and Mrs Payne's caravan was flattened. It was meant to be their last break of the summer; it turned out to be their last break ever, crushed to death by a lorry. Squashed in their sleep like road-kill. Poor Deirdre left harpooned on their ornamental railings, all 500 stone skewered like a lamb and mint kebab. This brave elephant (who was not scared of mice) would remember this day from the moment the emergency zoo transport arrived (equipped with stun gun.) To her dying day at Knowsley Safari Park.

'Fled from the scene' said witnesses of the dodgy lorry driver. He ran away, legged it, this slippery character. He had hidden his real name from the haulage company and would never be brought to justice for this accident (which he had always blamed on Deirdre). He kept this secret from the moment that Deirdre's trunk broke loose until his dying day in Curmudgeon Avenue. Yes, you heard right the dodgy driver turned out to be the notable Harold Goatshed, the nemesis of Edna Payne. The man who killed my beautiful Mr and Mrs Payne became my future resident.

(Safari parks ceased to commission cash in hand Cowboys after this).

Back in her hometown, Edna Payne was about to continue that same telephone conversation with a more concise version of what I have just told you. Edith continued to stare at her sister, her face as round as a dinner plate, her nose precisely pointed, her tiny mouth, now forming a little 'O' shape. After ten more minutes of elongated, 'I see's' and 'my goodness's' Edna was ready to terminate the phone call. She placed the bottle green receiver back in its base-unit and looked directly at Edith.

'Mother and Father are dead. They have been crushed to death by an elephant. An elephant on the way to Knowsley Safari Park' Edna remained standing to deliver this devastation. She was dressed all in black (a flattering colour), from her turtleneck to her knee-length stockings. Her upturned nose flared its nostrils aggressively to fend off the accumulating tears.

'What? Are you having a laff?' Edith blinked. She was dressed head to foot in floral patterns from her blouse, down to her elasticated knickers.

'No, Edith, I am not *'having a laugh'*. Our parents are dead, squashed by an elephant, they don't know who was driving the elephant-lorry, and I have to go and identify them.' As Edna spat her sentence, a string of snot escaped from her upturned nose. She grabbed her oversized handbag and slammed the frosted glass door behind her - then opened it again.

'Come on, Edith! Hurry up! ... And don't let the cat out!'

Chapter 3:   Return to Curmudgeon Avenue

A few short months after Mr and Mrs Payne were taken too soon (in their mid-nineties). Edna and Edith found themselves co-habiting in their parents' old house, returning to the same rooms they had occupied as youngsters. Edna lording it up in the attic room and Edith tucked away in one of the back bedrooms. (Do not worry Edith managed to claim the under-the-stairs cupboard for herself too). Number One Curmudgeon Avenue was, and will remain to be known locally as a sanctuary for grumpy geriatrics:

'Turn the heating off!

'Shut the door!'

'Answer the door!' The sisters barked at one another, and I was listening, of course, I was, I had no choice! They do say that walls have ears, don't they?

Edna and Edith had never really got on, *chalk and cheese* as the saying goes. Still, they were family, and they belonged to one another like stinging nettles and dock leaves. I remember when they were children. Edith had tripped Edna up (accidentally on purpose with her roller skates). Edna's breakfast of chocolate yoghurt, one hardboiled egg and burnt toast with blackcurrant jam flew into the air followed by the smell of acrid and sulphur. Edith had hidden in the under-the-stairs cupboard wishing that her older sister would be just a little more pleasant. She had waited in her hiding place listening to the heavy footsteps of Edna, leaving the house for Art College. As the two sisters wished each other dead, they somehow knew that they would be paired together again in their parents' Victorian terrace. One day in the future.

You may be wondering why these two sixty-something-year-old sisters did not have their own sorry houses to live in? It was all down to the cost of living these days. Mr and Mrs Payne's disagreeable daughters were both paupers and decided to move in, and conduct their romances, dramas and quarrels under my very nose. Well, I do not mind telling you all about it.

Edith had been married to Reg all her adult life, she felt like she had 'come home' when she met him. The North Manchester sky had been the colour of bruises on the day that Miss Edith Payne became Mrs Reginald Ricketts, the rain had soaked her wedding dress right through to her floral knickers. But they were in love, and they lived happily ever after. Reg had worked as a traffic warden and Edith, in the Citizen's Advice Bureau. It was a marriage made in Whitefield producing one son, Ricky Ricketts who grew up to be one of Britain's long term unemployed. In his job, Reg had often been asked *'How does he sleep at night?'* The answer, of course, was 'soundly and loudly'. During Edith and Reginald's marriage, to the outsider looking in, Reginald wore the trousers. He gave Edith a long list of things to do every single day (I told you she felt like she was coming home when she met him). But Edith maintained a little unconscious control. Over the years, the trousers that Reginald so proudly wore had literally got bigger and bigger. Edith was a feeder. Her long list of jobs naturally included making the evening meal (usually seventeen courses overindulged with calories). By the time Reg was in his fifties, he had become the only clinically obese traffic warden in the region. He died peacefully of a massive heart attack in his sleep during one Christmas day, *'soundly and loudly'*.

When Edith became a widow, she declined into financial difficulty. Her GP had automatically written out a two-week sick note, and her son Ricky Ricketts began to emotionally blackmail her for his (premature) inheritance. In addition to her personal problems, Edith feared the hard time that Pauline on the front desk was going to give her for being off sick. Pauline Foote was the shrewd and bossy administrator with her own set of rules and self-appointed seniority. On the day that Edith attempted to return to work, Ricky Ricketts sent his mother a text message demanding more cash. Edith started crying, and Pauline made it worse, using the authority afforded to her by the front desk, she sent Edith home again. Edith had to walk through reception with mascara-filled tears running down her face. The moment she stepped out onto the pavement, Edith was not just off sick; she was on the sick long term. And it was all Pauline's fault.

The personnel department had protocols and procedures to follow in this instance, but Pauline Foote made sure that she was interfering and involved when Edith tried to resolve the situation with a phone call.

'Citizen's Advice, Pauline speaking.'

'Hi Pauline, it's me, is that manager, David in today?'

'I'm sorry, I can hardly hear you, and could you speak up please?' Pauline barked down the phone.

'Sorry Pauline, it's me, Edith, I'm trying to find out if I can come back to work?'

'And where are you phoning from please?'

'Pauline! It's me! Edith! 'She looked around the

house that she did not usually see during the day 'I'm phoning from... err, my house!'

'I'm sorry; you are going to have to speak up! With whom is it you would wish to speak with?'

Edith was getting frustrated. She wasn't that quiet. There was something suspect about Pauline's tone; she had put on a false posh voice *'with whom is it that you wish to speak with?'* NOT YOU PAULINE, Edith thought.

Things continued in this manner until Edith was eventually sacked. I say sacked, I mean had her position terminated, retired on ill health. With no wage coming in, and Ricky Ricketts draining her bank balance, Edith could no longer afford the family home Reg and her doted on.

So when Edith's parents died, it was like all her Christmases had come at once. The sisters did try to sell me, but I had turned into a money pit which neither could afford to remedy.

As for Edna, her relationship with long-term partner Mme Genevieve Dubois ended. She was left with mounting legal debts from the court case involving Genevieve's adopted son, Matteo. That, I must insist is a story for another day.

Chapter 4: The Cost of Roofing These Days

On this particular day in Whitefield, the sky looked like an old bed sheet that had been caught up in the wash with a stray black sock one too many times.

'Edith!' Edna shouted her sister from the second-floor loft conversion where she looked down on the world.

'Yes,' Edith answered, with no intention of being heard in the under-the-stairs cupboard. Back upstairs, Edna knew exactly where her sister would be and continued to shout her.

'Edith! Fetch me that Agatha Christie I'm partway through, won't you? Oh, and make me a cup of tea. Strong with plenty of milk'...

'And two and a half sugars' Edith echoed her sister. She crawled out of her hiding place, put the kettle on and searched for Edna's novel in amongst the pile of newspapers. By the time she had climbed both flights of steep stairs and knocked on Edna's door which was now shut - (how rude!), the heavens had opened supplying another of August's heavy showers.

'Edna! I've made you a cup of tea, but I can't find that book you wanted...'

'Well, go and have another look then!' Edna bossed from the other side of the door.

'No! Two flights of stairs, Edna!'

'I know, Edith, I thought you would have lost a bit of weight after two weeks of living back here!' Edna insulted Edith, who rattled the door open. There was a bucket behind it, and one set on a table on the other side of the room. Water trickled out of the light fittings and bounced off the bottom of the bucket.

'The roof 's leaking!' Edith's nose pointed up to the ceiling and her mouth shaped into a visible 'O'.

'I know!' replied Edna. 'I haven't been able to start any of my nude self-portraits.' she opened another chocolate bar, and Edith ignored the artistic reference.

'Well, what are we going to do?'

'Oh for goodness sake Edith, grow up! You will have to get a roofer in.'

'Me? Why do I have to do it?'

'Look it's not a problem, Edith. Just look in the Yellow Pages, ring a roofer, and ask for a quote. It's quite simple' Edna was skilled at getting other people to do things for her.

'Well if it's so simple, why don't you do it?' Edith's décolletage became mottled pink with vexation.

'Edith,' Edna sat forwards on her bean bag in a patronising position. 'Your bedroom is nearest to the downstairs telephone. We both know that Mother and Father should have seen to this roof before they decided to die. The responsibility for the house has fallen to me, and I am delegating to you. So, hurry up, find us a roofer!'

And with that, Edith ran downstairs as fast as her little legs could carry her to the under-the-stairs cupboard. She lit one of her relaxation candles and breathed in deeply. On her next, exhale, she opened her wee eyes and saw the telephone directory. Who on earth still uses the *Yellow Pages*?

The following day, the situation with the Manchester weather had not improved, and Edith tramped up the stairs for the twentieth time. 'Edna, I've got three roofers coming around, one after the other to give us quotes about fixing this leak.'

'Carry on, Edith!' Edna waved her sister away from her space and started drawing on even more eyebrow. Back when Edna had begun associating with Mme Genevieve Dubois all those years ago, things changed for her. In her looks and her conceitedness, she had always bullied Edith though, that was not new.

'Oh! There's the doorbell!' Edith ran down the stairs, her cheap flip-flops conspired to trip her up. Wearing jeans moulded around the bottom portion of her hips that had not fit since the late nineteen-nineties. And due to her small stature, their hem now pulled her back onto the step she had just alighted. Well, she went arse over tit, didn't she?
Ding dong sounded the doorbell.
'Wait! Wait!' Edith tried to get up and rush to the front door. It was no good, she was winded like a broken Weeble, fighting to stand, unable to gain purchase on the threadbare carpet. 'Edna!' she shouted. 'Edna, please answer the door!'
But Edna was oblivious, pretending to read, but really watching YouTube clips of cats. After two more doorbells and a letterbox rattle, the roofer was gone. 'Oh no!' Edith sighed. One down, two to go. Edith was not going to get caught out this time. She carried one of the small pouffes from the front room and squashed it into the hall. There Edith sat staring at the door, reminding her of a time when she had done the very same thing as a girl. But back then, Edith had not been waiting for a roofer... Edith had waited for a Romeo to sweep her off her feet. A handwritten note was delivered one day, all those years ago, which read:

'Roses are red, violets are blue. Please look at me and say 'He'll do'. How about it, love? From Harold'

As a girl, this inappropriate letter had fired Edith's imagination. She had waited on that doorstep for the best part of a week until her father had chastised her, 'Prince Charming isn't going to just knock on the door, Edith!' The note turned out to be for Edna as it goes. My! Edith had not thought of those days until just now. She would not know Harold if she fell over him! Edith sat on the pouffe, wondering whatever happened to Harold. And did Edna ever think about him? Edith hardly dare ask! Hmmm ...

'Edith!' Edna shouted from upstairs, her voice muffled by Edith's imagination. 'Edith! Edith! Edith!' and so it went on until Edna was forced to take a break from her own self-importance and make her way downstairs to put the kettle on.

'I'm waiting here on the pouffe until the roofer comes' Edith asserted uncharacteristically, she was not being fooled this time.

'And I am going to the kitchen to make myself a black coffee.' Edna bossed with her everyday voice, the one she uses for everyday occasions. There was an angry banging on the glass pane at the top of the front door, and Edith jumped out of her skin. The palm of her left hand automatically landed on her décolletage, (a gesture she usually reserved for everyday anxiety).

'Is that the roofer, Edith?' Edna shouted over the sound of the kettle.

'Yes,' Edith said while hitching herself closer to the door on the pouffe.

'Well, tell him to use the door knocker! I get very annoyed by people who are incapable of using the correct utilities!'

'Yes,' Edith said, almost at the front door and still on the pouffe... (Why she did not just stand up and open the door is anyone's guess). The delay made the roofer repeat his erroneous greeting. Edith reached up to open the latched door, just a crack mind - the pouffe was now wedged in the vestibule, with Edith sat on top of it. Her little face, as round as a dinner plate, looked up towards the roofer.

'Hello!' he said 'Is your mum in?' he shouted through the crack in the door. She looked even smaller, squashed up in the vestibule.

'She's dead.'

'Dead?'

'Yes. Mother got squashed by an elephant.'

The roofer stood back and looked at the number on the sign to check he had the correct address.

'Did you phone me about having your roof looked at?' the roofer was getting confused now. Just then, Edna appeared in the scene. She pushed her sister out of the way, which was uncomfortable - with her being wedged in the vestibule. Edith fell backwards, horizontal for the second time in as many hours, with her feet still on the pouffe.

'We want a quote. A quote to have the roof replaced!' Edna declared, with flared nostrils, flab bulged in and out of her black outfit and costume jewellery jangling like tinnitus. The roofer took in the image before him. He had been in the business for decades. He could tell a job that he did not wish to take on just by looking, (usually at the roof itself, not typically the customers). And therefore employed a trick he reserves for everyday business management. The roofer stood back and looked up from the street in the direction of the roof of Number One Curmudgeon Avenue. He shook his head, sucked in a sharp breath, whistled and tutted. Then proceeded to verbally offer to replace the sisters' roof for three times the going rate.

'HOW MUCH!?' Edith shouted from her position on the floor.

'He said...' Edna thought that Edith had simply not heard, she turned to the roofer 'Is that the going rate?'

'Yes, I'll let you and...' he looked at Edith again ' your daughter? Think it over... give me a call back if you need me.'

'He seemed nice' Edith said, as Edna shut the door.

'We are going to wait for the next quote, Edith. And he did not seem nice!' Edna asserted with the conviction that she reserves for everyday bossiness.

Chapter 5: A Problem Shared is a Problem Halved.

After several more roofing quotes, a man who had knocked on the wrong door, and numerous enquiries as to how the sisters were acquainted. (Lovers? Mother and daughter? Cell-mates?) They managed to secure a promise of a new roof. But there began another problem; how to pay for it.

'Well, we could ask the roofer if we can pay in instalments' Edith offered. Her little voice making her sound as if she knew what she was talking about, (which she did not).

'Don't be ridiculous, Edith! This is not the Citizen's Advice! You can't just solve everything with payment plans! We will have to accept, that after this, Edith, we will be in...' (Edna loved drawing out points in conversations). 'FINANCIAL DIFFICULTY!' Edna's nostrils flared, she stood up and looked out of the window to make her point. Edith's fingers reached for the neckline of her top, as so often they did.

'Well, well, we'll just have to tighten our seatbelts!'

'What?' Edna sat down, her lips, with hair covered wrinkles curled around her top set of teeth.

'You know, tighten our seatbelts,'

'Seatbelts?'

'You know, Edna, *'tighten your seatbelts'* people say it when they need to save money.'

'You mean *'tighten our belts'*' Edna rolled her eyes at Edith, as so often she did.

'No, it's seatbelts, I've heard people say it.' Edith now launched into a whole list of how the sisters' could save money, this went on for quite some time

'We could even share bathwater!' Edith ended her list. Every idea Edith offered, Edna dismissed with aggressive ferocity.

'Well, no, no Edith,' (actually, it was Edna who ended Edith's penny-pinching tirade). 'We'll have to think of a way of accumulating an income, although I do think that eating beans on toast for an entire month is not going help. Especially compared to the money you give to your son!'

'My son? Edna! He's your nephew!'

'Well, I don't like him, never have. He was a smelly child and is now a disagreeable adult.'

'OH!' Edith ran away from Edna and hid away in the under-stairs cupboard. She took out her smartphone, and un-friended Edna on Facebook, knowing this would hit Edna where it hurts. What business was it of hers about Ricky Ricketts and all the money that Edith had given him? (Even though she too detested her own son with a passion).

Meanwhile, Edna was casing the joint, for possible money-making ideas. People often mock those who watch endless hours of reality television. Still, Edna had learnt a lot from those documentaries about the vacuous housewives *and* the one about the national baking industry. There were also programmes about how to make money. People would find items of antique jewellery, left behind by scatter-brained dead relatives, selling them on for vast amounts of money. Some would even be lucky enough to chance upon an expensive work of art and travel the world with the BBC to authenticate its provenance. Edna racked her brain. She thought of the picture of the Chinese dragon that Edith had hung on her bedroom wall as a child. She was scared of it then but now kept it in her under-the-stairs hiding place. Edna realised it was a print, and she was not about to disturb her sister's tantrum. Edna let Edith stew as she investigated any traces of leftover wealth in Curmudgeon Avenue.

Edith had also put her thinking cap on. As the stupid one of the two sisters, she decided to sleep on it. Having bored herself with social media, including photographs of people she hardly knew and a quiz about which *Game of Thrones* character you would marry (Edith got Varys!) She decided to call it a day, falling asleep watching quiz shows on catch-up TV.

The following morning, when the sky's colour was yet to be noticed, the sisters met in the kitchen for breakfast. Both brimming with excitement after 'tightening their (seat) belts' overnight.

'Edna! I don't know where it came from, but this morning, I woke up with a great idea! We could win some money on a TV quiz show!'

For many years, Edith had harboured the secret ambition of game show participation. Not bothered about winning, just the taking part. She dreamed of answering all the questions, flirting and cracking jokes with the presenter, making friends with the other contestants. Yes. Edith's guilty pleasure was TV quiz shows. She watched all the greats, '*Mastermind*'. '*The Chase*', '*Pointless*'. Edith had often planned to pluck up the courage and apply to appear on one of them. What better time than now! Now that they needed funds for the roof, funds to get the two of them out of financial difficulty! She could apply with her bossy, overbearing sister!

'Edith, you do realise they won't let you hide behind the furniture! And anyway, they don't want you wearing one of Mother's old nightdresses on television!' Edna, being the dominant of the two sisters, made fun of Edith.

Old nightdress? Edith looked down at her floral ensemble. This was not nightwear! It was what she had chosen to wear today, the day that she was awake and full of enthusiasm. Edna continued her harsh reasoning regarding the grand ambition of quiz show winnings, but it fell on deaf ears. Edith already imagined herself in the performance line of the camera; the quiz show contestants announcing themselves on screen:

'I'm Hilda, I'm a knitting pattern designer from Wakefield. Hi, I'm Veronica, I'm a dog groomer's receptionist from Kidderminster. Hi, I'm Michael I'm a candlestick maker from Welwyn Garden City...'

'Edith! EDITH!' shouted Edna, frightening Edith out of her daydream. 'My idea is much more practical, and therefore the one we are going with...' Edna smoothed down her mohair jumper over her funny shaped torso. 'Edith, we are going to get a lodger. A problem shared is a problem halved.' ...

But for me, a lodger means yet more nincompoops!

Chapter 6: What the Elephant Truck Driver Did Next.

One day during June in Radcliffe, an electric-storage-heater replacement salesman was followed by a Border terrier. It snapped at his heels. Eventually, Harold gave in and pulled out his lunch from his rucksack. Breaking his sausage roll in half, he fed it to the dog. Harold's next potential customer was Mrs Lomax. The dog seemed to know the address and got excited when Harold rang the doorbell...

'Ahhh you must belong to Maggie Lomax, little terror stealing my sausage roll!'

Margaret Lomax answered the door. She was not really in the mood for Harold, always making himself comfortable in her pristine front room. So she planned to talk to him in the hallway, and get rid quickly. Margaret tried to stop him, but Harold brushed past her in the hall.

'Hellooooo Margaret' the dog followed Harold into Margaret's front room. Margaret rolled her eyes to the ceiling.

'Come in, Harold. What are you selling this time?' she said '*and why the bloody hell are you bringing that dog around with you!'* she thought; because Margaret would never say a swear word out loud. Harold made himself at home on Margaret's front room settee, as did the dog, curling up on the Persian rug. Margaret was very house proud, her front room being her pride and joy.

'Wait until you see the special offer I've got for you' Harold's head wobbled 'Special electric storage heaters.'

'What!?' Margaret gasped.

'Yes, I'm selling these in this area only, especially for you.'

'Especially for me?'

'Yes, special, special offer.'

'Harold' Margaret pointed out of her Radcliffe window 'It's June!'

'I know!'

'It's the hottest June on record.'

'I know!' Harold really was a smug git.

'The flags are cracking out there!'

'I know!' Harold was at risk of being beaten up in Radcliffe by Margaret Lomax, the retired widow.

'Well if you know *Harold* then what the *bloody hell* (she whispered those two words) do you think I want to buy an electric storage heater for?'

'Ahh, that's why they are on special offer because no one will want to buy them in the summer!'

'You think?'

There was not a lot Harold could do with that, except continue the hard sell.

'Yes, it will work out cheaper for you in the long run, see I'm also selling solar panels for your roof. So, (Harold sniffed) by the time you need to use the heaters, the cost of running them will be free.' Harold continued, and Margaret was fuming. 'Here, let me show you' Harold was about to open his briefcase and show Margaret a convoluted break down of facts and figures. The lid was firmly snapped shut on his slippery fingers. This was Margaret's doing, and she did not look happy.

'Harold. What makes you think I want to buy something now that I don't need so that I can buy something else that will expunge the cost of my original purchase?' Margaret, who never swears out loud, had an excellent vocabulary for a widow from Radcliffe. Harold was flummoxed, Margaret had the upper hand, and there was no way that Harold was going to style his way out of it.

'I just thought you might want to save a bit of money in the winter months, I know how cold it gets in Radcliffe.' being Harold, he would not give up.

'I might not make it to winter, Harold! Your mother didn't, God rest her soul' Margaret crossed herself, even though she was not Catholic and had not seen the inside of a church for quite some time. Margaret, like most of her counterparts at MECCA Bingo on Bolton Road, feared the onset of winter, even in June.

'Yes, I forget how close you were to my mother' Harold lied, and slightly pushed his bottom lip out. Truth be told, he was trying to stretch out the conversation. Margaret was not for offering him a cuppa and a Kit-Kat like she usually did. Harold looked around Margaret's house. The Persian rug, the Toby Jugs lined up on the shelf. Everything was perfect, apart from the scruffy little dog lying on his back, looking out of place and grinning at both humans.

'So, when did you get this puppy, Margaret?' Harold said.

Margaret's eyes widened 'That's not my dog!' she edged further away with alarm 'I thought you had started bringing your dog round with you. I didn't really want to invite it in, but it followed you!'

Harold's mouth was wide open, but no words were coming out... Harold thought the dog belonged to Margaret, and Margaret thought the dog belonged to Harold.

Then it happened... In slow motion...
The dog stood up and stretched its front paws. It
shook out its fur. It looked at Harold and Margaret
with that look that dogs do, as if it was falling in love
with them... Then it squatted down and two curly
brown ones popped out from under its tail. They
landed neatly on Margaret Lomax's Persian rug.

'Noooooooo, NO, NO. Noooooooooooo! Get out!
Get out!... Ahhhhhhhhh' Margaret screamed. She
started hitting Harold with a cushion whipped from
the settee. Harold did try to explain and offered to
clean up, but it was too late for that. Margaret was
threatening to dial 999. The dog ran out of the front
door, never to be seen again. Harold also felt like
running, but Margaret was busy slamming the door in
his face. She decided against calling the emergency
services with a dog poop emergency. After the mess
had been neatly scooped up and thrown into next
door's back yard, she calmly phoned the storage
heater company to put in an official complaint about
Harold.

The story went down in history in the office.

Harold was called in for a severe telling off. He
had to pay for Margaret's rug to be cleaned. Harold
had the cheek to try and argue that the incident was
partly Margaret's fault. All this modern business of
self-employment and zero-hour contracts, Harold's
door-to-door salesman days were short-lived, just
like his lorry driving job.

Chapter 7: Lodger Wanted.

Mrs Ali from the corner shop had a touch of the entrepreneur about her. This started when a stray bit of passing trade asked her for a jar of dried coriander. Having no such culinary condiments in stock, she had given the customer a few sprigs of her own, homegrown, fresh and fragrant. The customer had seemed surprised yet uncomfortable that there was no charge for this. Her embarrassment had shoed herself out of the most popular shop in Whitefield, without making any legitimate purchases. This was the last time Mrs Ali gave anything away for free. And now every window in her Victorian terrace on the corner of Curmudgeon Avenue adorned a window box, each with its very own herb farm. Not an inch of that shop went begging, including the left front window. For a small charge or 'commission', Mrs Ali allowed her customers to advertise sales or services (nothing salacious of course). Another small charge was levied, should the advertise-ee not have their own little piece of card to create their flyer with. It was free to borrow a pen.

There are two types of people in this world; those that look at the sky, and those who look at the street. Fear of treading in dog muck is a real thing. Edith is the type of person who looks down when walking along, so on this day was unable to take note of the sky on the short journey to Mrs Ali's corner shop.

'Hello, Mrs Ali. I've come to put a sign in your window.' Edith said, pinching the coins required for this transaction, which Mrs Ali accepted, and why should she not? The notice cards partially obstructed her view of the street. Being naturally nosy, this was a considerable sacrifice. Edith wrote down the advert for the lodger, as Edna had ordered - I mean instructed.

'LODGER WANTED *Two later-life sisters require a house guest to share their lovely home with. Going rate, amenities included (within reason).*

'There' Edith said, Edna had suggested adding *'within reason'* to the notice. She had read all about ne'er-do-wells renting rooms for the cultivation of cannabis farms. This would increase the electricity bill at Curmudgeon Avenue, rather than pay for the roof. Describing themselves as *'later*-life', Edna thought would attract a desirable class of people. Edith added their telephone number and popped the card in its little plastic sleeve, amongst notices for bicycles and beds for sale, *'cleaner wanted'* and *'cleaning services'.*

'Oh, Mrs Ali, I've had an idea! These two cards can help each other out!' Edith loved to meddle, and there was an endless supply of idiots, it seemed who could not manage their own lives. She placed the cards carefully on the counter. 'He wants a cleaner, and she wants to work as one! They just need to be introduced!'

'Oh, no... no... no. These two darling advertisers already know each other.' Mrs Ali shook her head as she had already dealt with this moment of serendipity. 'This is the ex-husband' she held up the 'cleaning service' card. 'And this is the ex-wife' Mrs Ali put the back of her hand to the side of her mouth 'slovenly' she nodded at Edith, who refused to accept this defeat.

'Well then, they were made for each other! He is

clean, and she is... filthy! Opposites, like Jack Spratt and his wife!'

'Who?'

'Never mind' said Edith, returning the cards to their original location, after kissing them both together. 'Oh, I almost forgot to buy a tin of peas!' today was day three of Edith's money-saving menu.

'Thank you, Edith, and don't forget to renew your fee every month, for the advert!' Mrs Ali said, making a record in one of her many little notebooks.

When Edith arrived home, it was three twenty in the afternoon, she had not been gone long of course.

'I'm hungry, what did you buy us for dinner?' Edna asked. Edith put the tin on the table. 'Peas! Peas, Edith? A tin of peas! We can't just have a tin of peas between us for dinner!' Edna had dismissed her Mancunian accent some years ago and was now posh. Too posh to eat peas for her evening meal. If she was honest, peas were no good for her flatulence problem, Edith should know that! Edna could not stop farting and had a constant battle avoiding wind inducing foods. The other thing that Edna liked to avoid was paying for unnecessary things. Having to pay to put a notice in Mrs Ali's window? *I'm not paying!* Edna decided to have a word with Mrs Ali, her neighbour.

'Edith, I'm going to go and have a word with Mrs Ali. Our neighbour. We should not have to pay to have advertisements in windows, not if we are neighbours!'

'Oh! It was only pence!'

'It's the principle!' Edna looked at herself in her mirror 'I just need to put my face on, before I go outside!' Edna refused to leave the house without makeup. 'It won't take me two ticks.' An hour or two after declaring she was going out, Edna was ready. Having painted on expensive makeup (bought before entering into financial difficulty). She shaped her face, lashed those eyelashes and plumped those lips all for the sake of less than a pound. It was almost going dark when Edna ventured down Curmudgeon Avenue to the most popular shop in Whitefield, and the sky looked like a hazelnut Quality Street. Edith, like a discontinued variety, watched Edna walk away with sturdy strides ...

'Oh!' Edna looked at the notice in Mrs Ali's window. 'There must be some mistake!' Edna initially blamed Edith, she could never spell. Edith's handwriting had been tampered with on the notice, and now it was a different type of advert altogether. 'Lodger wanted' now read 'tODGER WANTED!' Oh! The disgust and dismay! Edna could not remember the last time she wanted a todger! She could not speak for her sister but was confident that Edith would not advertise for such a thing in a corner shop window. Someone had graffiti-ed their notice and sullied their intentions. Edna felt violated and was not about to stand for it.

'Mrs Ali! Have you seen what has happened to our notice?!'

'Hello to you too, Edith/Edna!' (Mrs Ali regularly mixed the sisters up). She took the notice from Edna and started reading it. Her eyes bulged at the word 'todger.' Blushing briefly, an amusing, entrepreneurial thought struck her 'It's extra for that type of advert!' she nudged Edna, who was not amused.

'More money? I don't think I should have to pay *any* money! We are neighbours, and now, someone has tampered with our advert! Did you see who did it?'

'No, but I did see several men take down your telephone number; most popular advert of the day, in this popular corner shop!'

Edna stroked the back of her ear with her forefinger. She was not used to compliments, no matter how far-fetched. Her smile turned into the ugly realisation that she was being made fun of. She huffed, re-wrote the advert and hoity-toitied her way out of the shop.

'I'll give you the next month free!' Mrs Ali shouted after Edna... *but I don't think you'll need it!* She chuckled to herself.

Samantha Henthorn

Chapter 8: Meanwhile, In Radcliffe.

Harold's goggly eyes darted about under his spectacles, he smacked his lips together, and his neck wobbled like a turkey.

'Bedroom tax! Bedroom tax!' he spat, as he read the pub's newspaper to himself 'Well, they do say that we are all only six steps away from being homeless.'

The Bridge Tavern, the finest pub in the centre of Radcliffe was the town's Winchester. That is to say, that should there be an apocalyptic incident, The Bridge is where the residents of Radcliffe would accumulate, (in the same way as a popular film about Zombies). Harold often treated himself to a pint and a read of the papers. You would not be mistaken for thinking that Harold actually *enjoyed* getting his knickers in a twist over whatever repetitive news story caught his eye. He ordered his second pint.

'Making that one last, Harold?' from the safety of behind the bar, Trisha was very friendly with all the customers. She could not help being a little offhand with Harold, though. He never tipped and always looked over the top of his glasses at her. He was the type that Trisha's older brother had warned her against when she got the job. She adjusted her top, suddenly becoming conscious of her cleavage.

'Scuse me' a brutish bearded bloke pushed Harold off his stool, Harold grabbed hold of the bar, which in turn, knocked his pint over.

'Excuse *you*!' Harold outraged. The bloke ignored Harold and mumbled his order at Trisha through his beard. It was all pints and shots. Then he asked for some Rizzla papers, Harold made a scoffing noise.

'You say summat?' Demanded the bearded bloke.

Harold's face reddened, he coughed, and his newly shaky hands fluttered with the newspaper.

'It's ok, he was just coughing' Trisha said, unconvincingly. Now, this was the type of bloke that her brother should have warned her about. She handed the brute his change, who then held on to Trisha's hand for longer than was reasonably necessary, caressing her palm with his work-shy fingers. He left the two red faces at the bar and went to join his mates who downed their drinks, punctuated by manly exclamations.

'Time, everyone, please!' Tricia shouted. Harold's heart thumped in his chest. He felt woozy as he stood up... His heart plummeted towards his feet...

'WATCH OUT HAROLD!' Tricia thought Harold was going to fall 'You look like you've seen a ghost!' she steadied his arm. It was closing time anyway so Harold went outside for some fresh air... I knew that Tricia fancied me, Harold thought to himself. Serving me up a full pint of beer instead of the shandy I asked for! The little minx met her type before, trying to get me drunk! Harold, of course, had not met Tricia's kind before. He had asked for a shandy, but she had served him up watered down slops when he was not looking.

'I'll put you in your grave, mate!' the bearded bloke said, having waited outside for Harold. A noise came out of Harold's mouth, which was neither neutral nor forgiving. The bearded bloke clutched Harold around the upper quarter of his coat, dragging him near to his bearded face. It was then, eye to eye, in the night light that Harold could tell that the bearded bloke could only be in his early twenties.

'The cheek of it!' Harold protested. The bearded

bloke dropped Harold, throwing him against the pub sign. He pointed at one of his mates.

'See 'im?' Harold had to look, 'See 'im, he's Psycho Steve' Harold said nothing. The bloke's eyes were now touching Harold's spectacles, expectant of an apology or show of misguided respect from Harold. Psycho Steve approached Harold; he could not allow his name to be shunned. He started what he and the bearded bloke had set out to do that night, what Harold would be unable to finish. Harold was thrown to the floor, their actions punctuated by laughter. Through adrenalin-filled squirms, Harold saw the wheels of a car pull up; his plea of rescue was quashed by the sight of a pair of trainers. The trainers walked over to the pub entrance, initially ignoring Harold's misfortune. The trainers stopped and dropped a cigarette butt. Good! They have noticed what's going on! The trainers walked over to Harold, wait! That's not right! Are they going to join in? Can't you see I'm out-numbered?! (As if Harold could have taken the bearded bloke!) Then the trainers spoke.

'Steve! I've not seen you for time!'
Harold sat up and saw another twenty-something man bumping fists, not with 'Psycho Steve' but with the original instigator, the bearded bloke. Are they both called Steve? Psycho Steve and Sleeveless Steve?

'This is my mate, 'Psycho Steve.' the bearded bloke thumbed towards the other Steve, who let go of Harold and walked towards the new man, and shook his hand.

'I've just come to pick my sister up, she works behind the bar here' Trisha's trainer-wearing brother said.

'Oh, I've seen her, she's tidy!' grinned Sleeveless

Steve.

'Watch it!' Trainers dismissed with a laddish laugh 'I won't let her get a taxi, I'm not letting *you* near her!'

Harold's protest of: 'I-have-just-been-assaulted!' were drowned by laughter, stiletto heels and car engines. That was the trouble with Harold; he always wanted to have the last word. Standing up, he flapped towards Trisha. 'Aren't you going to do something? Don't you think you should call the police?'

'Huh?' Trisha said one foot already in her brother's car.

'Do one Grandma!' the Steve's turned on Harold, who himself turned and ran. He was running for his life, all the way home. All the way to his mother's old house. The house he grew up in. Running in lace-up weasel shoes resembling shiny tan mice. How fast could he run in these? His arms outstretched his palms braced for the door. Harold turned and noticed something, a pristine BMW parked right outside, like borrowed pomposity. Raindrops patterned randomly on the bonnet, a reminder of Radcliffe. His neck made a loud cracking sound, and he skidded directly inside.

Who is that parked outside my house? Harold thought. Of course, he didn't own the street, he owned the house (although, that in itself was another matter). The last time he had driven was the elephant incident, and so he had no need for the parking space. Thinking of the last time, he had driven reminded him of Morecambe Bay, his sister, and childhood trips to the seaside. The gentile ambience, bracing winds and stiff upper lip made Harold's mother lose her Radcliffe swagger and adopt fanciful airs with a matching posh voice. For example, she was always telling Harold she had named him as such because 'A fancy name costs nothing.'

Harold adopted his mother's uppity airs presuming that he was better than his older sister, because he had been named after royalty, and she was called Sharon. They were children, of course at the seaside and the siblings had not seen each other since their mother's funeral. Harold opened the door, something was different, there was a smell of perfume, a light left on in the kitchen. Harold strode towards it, turning it off before bed. He almost stumbled over a woman's shoe, pointed, polished, proud, although stunted, like a puffin's beak. The shoe dangled off a woman's crossed leg. Harold stopped in shock at the sight; he was not alone.

'Hello Harold' the pointy shoe said.

Chapter 9: It's Alright For Some.

'Sharon' Harold said, his jaw set like he meant it. He knew why she was here, the matter of his mother's house but had to ask: 'Why are you here? And how did you get in?'

'It's Shania now, Harold. I changed my name by Deed Poll. You know why I'm here, and as for how I got in, I have a key, you idiot.'

'Well, you could have just telephoned!'

'I've been trying to contact you, Harold! You have not answered any of my messages. For goodness sake, I haven't seen you since Mother's funeral.'

'I've been busy! And anyway, it's not *Deed Poll,* its D-Poll!'

'No, it isn't its Deed Poll! I should know! Anyway, busy! Ha! Doing what? Oh don't bother Harold, I don't want to know. I just want to sort this out, once and for all.' Sharon's angry Radcliffe accent had reappeared. That was the trouble with Harold, he was so annoying even his own sister could not be in the same room as him for more than five minutes without coming out in vexation. Harold started waffling on with himself about where he got the incorrect term 'D-Poll' from (proof by repeated assertion was another one of his annoying traits). Harold knew nothing! Their mother's funeral had been a bone of contention that remained unpicked. Sharon had paid for the wake, a slap-up do buffet of sausage rolls and sandwiches. Harold had been first in the queue with his paper plate, and last to offer to pay for it. In fact, he never offered. Sharon smirked to herself when she remembered that Harold took a box of leftovers home, some of which had been on the floor. She felt a little mean for finding this amusing, but then, it was Harold. Now, here he was, having not put their mother's house up for sale, living rent-free.

'I can't afford to sell it, Sharon. I've just been reading about the bedroom tax. There are three bedrooms if you include your old box-room, imagine how much that will set me back?!'

'You idiot, Harold, bedroom tax is not about how many bedrooms you have in a house that you own! Anyway, it's inheritance tax you should be worried about, although without looking into it, and without knowing the valuation, Oh Harold, we need to get on with it before...'

Harold's neck was taking some punishment tonight! He whipped around quickly, and was that the start of a smile? 'Before what Sharon? Are you dying?' he said.

'No, Harold, I'm not dying. I am going to live in Australia. I'm emigrating.'

'Emigrating!' Harold's neck adopted a wobbly life of its own.

'Yes, Kevin and myself, we have decided we are sick of the rat race, so we have sold up, and we hope to leave in the next six months.'

'Rat-race? You mean he finally left his wife!' Harold asked a personal question which Sharon ignored.

'Yes, they are a bit more relaxed in Australia.'

'You say that as if you're getting a bus to Bolton! Pah! Life's the same wherever you live.'

'It's been my dream since I was a child' Sharon dramatised.

'No, it hasn't.'

'Yes, it has, Harold.'

'No, I remember, you wanted to be a showjumper. Like on *National Velvet.*'

Sharon dismissed unpleasant memories of Harold getting a deluxe magician's kit and her receiving a second-hand hobby horse for Christmas. She replaced those thoughts with the matter in hand.

'Harold, I want to tie up any loose ends before I go, so move out, so that I can sell up!'

'No.' Harold folded his arms and looked straight ahead, as though Sharon was not there.

'What do you mean 'No'? You have to! I'm entitled!' Sharon stood angrily in the dark, trying to explain to her brother. Harold did not move for longer than was reasonably necessary. Eventually, Sharon left, stealing some of her brother's post on her way, how foolish of him to leave unopened envelopes at the door!

'Entitled? Well, it's alright for some!' Harold said to himself, no one will want to buy this house! It's in Radcliffe! And with that, Harold decided to stay put.

Samantha Henthorn

Chapter 10: Toonan and Wantha.

'What's that smell?! Pooh! Edith, it smells like cheese and onion pie. *Off* cheese and onion pie! Egh, it's stinging my nose! What is it?' Edna had been interrupted. She had heard the doorbell, of course, but Edith would have answered it. That was some time ago, but time enough for the sickly gas to make its way upstairs. Edna covered her nose and mouth with her turtleneck jumper, pulling the skin underneath her eyes downwards, revealing her big eyes with mascara clumped eyelashes. She dropped the jumper revealing a downturned disgusted nose at the sight of a young woman sitting with Edith at the kitchen table.

'Oh... hello' Edna said, glancing at Edith. The young woman would have thought this unfortunate expression was a family trait, as Edna and Edith's faces now matched with identical disgust. She stood up and shook Edna's hand, without her consent, her own hand rough and clammy.

'I'm Toonan, pleased to meet you' the young woman said, running her fingers through her greasy hand-dyed hair, complete with hints of summer adventures. Her tracksuit top rustled, the elastic around the waist having not quite captured her midriff.

'Toonan has come about the room' Edith pleaded, hoping Edna would shoo this young woman away.

'Oh!' Edna said, the turtleneck was around her face again. 'That's an unusual name, where's it from?'

'I dunno, my mum made it up' Toonan circled her finger next to her right temple. 'She was a bit mental back then, all those pills she took.'

'Pills?' barked Edna.

'Was there something wrong with her?' Edith concerned.

'You could say that.' Toonan's face erupted into a toothless smirk. The two sisters hardly dared to speak, because speaking meant breathing, and breathing involved inhaling this young woman's malodorous presence. Edna left the room; sneakily shouting through the door that she was otherwise engaged (meaning that she was pretending to use the bathroom). Edith pulled all her citizen's advice knowledge from the back of her mind to handle this.

'I'm sorry we are not taking benefits.'

'Eh?' Toonan said.

'No social.' Edith said 'We are not accepting housing benefit for rent.'

'I'm not on benefits, you cheeky cow!' laughed Toonan, half affronted, half dismissing.

'Oh' gasped Edith, searching her brain for another excuse like searching for lost keys in a handbag.

'I work me.' Toonan shoved the arms of her tracksuit top up towards her elbows, revealing regrets of tattoos, crossed out and coloured again. 'I work nights.'

'Oh, what line of work are you in?'

'If she works nights, tell her she won't be able to come home in the middle of the night, it might wake me up, or scare the cat. Tell her Edith!' shouted Edna from the other side of the kitchen door. 'Ohhh' Edna jumped when she noticed a silhouette of a person with an enormous head at the front door. The big head rattled the door knocker.

'Alright,' the big head said, who turned out to have big hair, big afro hair. She looked Edna up and down, making a clicking sound with her tongue and the roof of her mouth.

'Alright, sis! This is Wantha, my sista.'

'You don't look like sisters!' Edna said, smiling her gummy smile. She had a special voice she reserved for when she was trying to fit in with young people. Edith noticed this and frowned in confusion at Edna. Her face exhausted with all the tales of disgust and disorientation.

'Oh, yeah *sista* I get you' Edna said, shifting her shoulders and flicking her hair with immediate and inappropriate fake streetwise speak.

'Edna!' Edith gasped in disapproval.

'What! We are sisters!' said Toonan 'Different dads' she said nodding. Different *mums* too, thought Edna, dropping her foolish street attitude.

'Don't worry, I'll make sure she doesn't make much noise when we come in, I heard what you were saying when I was stood at your door.' Wantha clicked her tongue at Edna again. Toonan started picking up Edith's post from the table, a subscription to *Woman's Weekly*, a credit card statement and a letter from the dentist about a missed appointment. Toonan's nosiness was nearly as bad as her body odour. Edith's top lip curled around the top of her teeth, which in turn were perched in disgust on her bottom lip. She reached out and snatched the post out of Toonan's greasy hand.

'Oi! Snatchy!' Toonan said. 'It was the name, Ricketts that caught my eye.' Toonan's tone was now one of mischief, smirking at her sister.

'Ricketts?! Do you... no, you can't' Wantha shook her large afro in disbelief. 'I knows someone called Ricketts.' she could not bear to say his name, but could not resist testing the water. Edith, on the other hand, guessed that Wantha was talking about her son, Ricky Ricketts. Although Ricky only spoke to his mother when he wanted something (money), Edith retreated to the role of proud school-playground-mum. Delighting in the knowledge that their child had made friends.

'You must mean my son, Ricky Ricketts!' Edith gushed, immediately changing her mind about Wantha and imagining her as a daughter in law. But Wantha was not impressed. Edna meanwhile did not know what to do with this exchange and stood frozen with her gummy grin.

'Don't you come to me, lady. Your boy is Ricky Ricketts? What kind of woman raises a freeloader?' Wantha was an outrage of afro hair, fake nails and tongue doing all kinds of clicking. She too, it seemed had a special voice she reserved for moments like this. Toonan was wetting herself with laughter in the corner.

'A what, love?' Edith was flummoxed.

'Click!' Wantha looked at Edith with the disgust she had felt towards Ricky Ricketts when he dumped her unceremoniously. Without bothering to tell her, and not before emptying her bank balance. 'Come on Toonan, we can't live here, not with the stink of Ricky Ricketts hanging around.' Wantha moved towards the back door, swinging her hips and oversized behind purposefully with every step.

'But I thought the room was for you, Toonan... ew, my days!' Edith inhaled a full gasp of Toonan's odour. *Never mind saying my son stinks!*

'That's made my day!' Toonan laughed, shaking her head, she patted Edith on the forearm, leaving the two strange sisters from Curmudgeon Avenue.

'Benefit scroungers!' Edna said, returning to her normal disgusted voice.

'They said they worked nights... and the tall one was friends with my Ricky!'

'What do you think 'working nights' means? And as for Ricky, oh I never did like him!'

'I don't like him either Edna, but he is my son! Pass me that air freshener will you?'

'What's for tea?' said Edna passing her sister the can of lavender spray 'And don't say cheese and onion pie!'

Chapter 11: Homes Under the Hammer.

To grow up with a mother who preferred your brother and a brother like Harold told the tale of Shania (previously Sharon) Goathed's persuasive nature. Her puffin-pointed shoes had walked all six steps of Harold's homelessness, but without his knowledge. Shania Corral Goatshed had managed to persuade the solicitor, the estate agent and the house auction people that her brother, Harold, who she cared for (in his *condition)*; Had signed the house over to her. The house was then swiftly put on the market via an auction, and sold quicker than they could put a 'For Sale' sign up. It was easy; Harold's use of fake names over the years had made him almost invisible. Easy for Sharon, good at persuasion, she had already persuaded her boyfriend's wife, Georgina Foote to leave him by activating a campaign of cyberbullying. Thus freeing the two of them to move to Australia. That, of course, is another story, a good one, but I must insist it is saved for another day because we are here to find out why Harold needed to look for somewhere new to live.

Sharon did have the option to allow Harold to become a sitting tenant, she was told. But no, 'I'll make sure my brother is taken care of' she had smiled at the solicitor. Convincing smiling, something Sharon had learnt as a child when developing her powers of persuasion. She learned from the best, her brother Harold. And what he had demonstrated to her in childhood was coming back to bite Harold in the bum. Enter *Homes Under the Hammer.*

'And now here we are in Radcliffe, Greater Manchester with Lenny and Morgan first time buyers who bought this property at auction, for just over the reserve price.'

'CUT' shouted the smoking director.

The presenter was handed a takeaway coffee and huffed into the trailer. 'Which one is Lenny and which one's Morgan?' he could be heard whining. Lenny and Morgan were left standing at the front door of Harold's mother's house. It was now their house; they had the keys and the contracts and everything. The next scene was shot inside. Lenny and Morgan grinned nervously while the TV presenter forced open a window.

'Phew! Wow, it did say on the spec that the place needs some alterations, Lenny and Morgan will need to get rid of this smell too! It smells like socks and compost in here!'

Each scene ended with an overly cheesy grin from the cheesy presenter. The TV camera swept around the house while the presenter took the piss out of the furniture *'left behind by the previous owners'*. The final scene followed the usual format, where the grinning presenter would grill the new owners about renovation budgets and the predicted future of the house.

'Really? You think fifteen thousand pounds will be enough?' the presenter shook his head, looking around the ceilings of the house like a professional.

'Yes, that's all we've got, and anyway, Lenny will be doing most of the work himself, won't you Lenny?'

'Yeah' gruffed Lenny, who was not enjoying the presenter's tone.

'Well, as long as you don't blow the budget on cushions, you should be alright, hey, Morgan!' The presenter slapped Morgan on the arm, and then wiped his hand on his jeans. 'Next, we are off to Shoreditch to meet Tarquin and Delilah, who have just bought an old rectory.' the presenter fixed his grin, but there was no instruction from the film crew. They could see something that Lenny, Morgan and the presenter could not see.

'I can't hold my face in this stupid grin for much longer' the presenter said through gritted teeth. Behind him was something that had never been caught on camera before, not on '*Homes Under The Hammer*' anyway. Chemically enhanced hair, a shock of aubergine in the sunlight rose up from behind the orange settee followed by a pair of black-rimmed rectangular spectacles. A stubborn nose and lip licker's dermatitis lips introduced BBC daytime viewers to Harold.

'Excuse me,' he said with nasal tones. 'This is my house.'

Chapter 12: Meanwhile, on Curmudgeon Avenue.

Things were really not going well in Edith and Edna's search for a todger. I mean a lodger. Wantha and Toonan were the first of a long line of unsuitable potentials. There was the woman Edna was convinced she had seen on the reality TV eviction programme. Then there was the man Edith thought had a liking to one of the mug-shots of local '*Wanteds*' from the local paper. Then there was the family and their belongings squashed into checked launderette bags. It took all of Edna's posh voice strength to explain that the room was for single occupancy only and 'For goodness sake! Please stop unpacking your chattels!'

Of course, Ricky Ricketts heard on Wantha's grapevine that his mother had a room up for rent. He appeared on a day where the sky looked like porridge from behind the frosted glass of the vestibule in Curmudgeon Avenue. Skies, of course, do not really look like porridge, unless we are talking about the horizon on one of Edna's paintings. A painting that she painstakingly continued with, when she heard Ricky Ricketts' voice.

'I need you to transfer two hundred quid into my account. Otherwise, I'm gonna be overdrawn. I can't tell the bank it's my mum's fault, can I?'

'Right... I've told you, stop looking over my shoulder when I'm on the internet banking Richard!' Edith's shaky little voice was observed by Edna upstairs. She would not come down, though. She hated her nephew and scolded her sister for being so soft with him. Edna continued to paint her picture of a lumpy sky in cheap acrylic. (White paint is most likely to run out first, and Edith had Edna on a strict budget still because of the roof don't forget). Yes, the sky painting would not be finished until Ricky had left, and the roof fund had been transferred to his current account. It was too cold for naked self-portrait painting unless she put the heating on. But that would mean more expense and more risk of bumping into Ricky Ricketts. Edna continued painting. She opened the skylight out wide to take in inspiration of the outside world of Curmudgeon Avenue, Whitefield on this miserable Saturday. She observed two cars passing each other on the road below. Sliding around like the sausages in a tin of *Beans and Sausages*, gliding and almost colliding slowly. Slowly enough for the drivers of each car to glance recognition at one another before speeding off in opposite directions. Unbeknown to Edna, or Edith, (still held hostage by her son downstairs), these two mystery drivers were two more potential tenants of Curmudgeon Avenue. Both driving away before either had the chance to examine the built-in wardrobe or the stained glass window of the prospective rental. Both, subject of a misunderstanding meaning neither wanted to be in each other's company, let alone risk having to house share with each other.

Cassie Hunt and Sophia Levis were the longstanding victims of Whitefield gossip. From the fine establishments of the Northern Crafthouse and the several Italian restaurants on the main road to the Frigate pub of the Hillock estate, everyone knew their names. Some years ago, Sophia and Cassie were linked by a love interest. Cassie had dated Ryan since high school, but when Ryan moved into a shared house as a student, Sophia rolled into one of the adjacent rooms. Cassie and Ryan grew apart, and it was only a matter of time (but a respectable amount of time to young lovers) before Sophia and Ryan became an item. They were known to the Whitefield crowd as 'Rophia', a name that never had a ring to it. So much so that their relationship did not last. But the talk did. This all happened fifteen years ago, Ryan had since found his true self and was now in a relationship with Simon, but still, the gossip remained.

It was felt, within the Whitefield gossip, that Ryan and Sophia had not left a long enough gap between relationships. The more the whispers got around, the more exaggeration of overlap was added. This was never the case, of course. But Cassie and Sophia became what is known in Whitefield as a 'presumed enemy'. When their mutual friends got married, either Cassie or Sophia would be invited. Cassie would be invited to the Halloween party, and Sophia would be invited to the Bonfire, and so on. Even when Mrs Ali's mother died, and all of Whitefield was welcomed to her funeral, Cassie and Sophia were kept in separate rooms, without their knowledge, (or consent). There is nothing much else to gossip about than each other in those parts. So when both women needed a new place to live, and both drove down opposite ends of Curmudgeon Avenue, they recognised one another immediately.

'I hope that *stupid cow*' isn't moving in here!' Cassie said to herself in her car.

'I hope that *f'kng loser* isn't looking 'round the house I want to move into' said Sophia in her car. Both women lip-read each other's sentiments and sped off in opposite directions away from Curmudgeon Avenue. Away from Edna and Edith, inside Curmudgeon Avenue wondering why finding a todger was so very complicated.

Chapter 13: Harold's Dirty Protest.

Harold got to the bottom of his sister Sharon; I mean Shania's conniving, lying and manipulating. She pretended and persuaded others to believe that Harold had agreed to the sale of his mother's home, right from underneath his smelly feet! This put Harold in a right old pickle, as he had been claiming all sorts of benefits from that address. Including his dead mother's pension (for a while).

Harold visited the housing department to declare himself destitute. There he met a portly, fair-haired female called Keeley Brimstone, who provided Harold with a housing interview. She was not paying Harold much heed, sending emails at the same time as speaking to him at her desk. Emails, that Harold observed contained long lines of exclamation marks at the end of her sentences, such as '!!' The effect of which was surely irritating rather than useful. Harold drifted into memories of his days at Radcliffe Tech, *Radcliffe Technical College*, that is. They would never have stood for such poor displays of grammar. Then Keeley Brimstone said something which surely was down to poor education and inadequate grammar, she made a phrase up.

'So, you are homeless, but not roofless.'

'Pardon?'

'You have a roof over your head, so you are not really homeless.' Keeley said while pressing down on the 'Shift!' keys on her keyboard.

'What? Pardon, young woman! I am being kicked out of my own home by my sister! She has sold the property without my say so! I want to live in *Whit-field* and as you are the housing department I expect your assistance.'

'Whit-field?' asked Keeley Brimstone.

'Whit-field, yes that's where I intend to move to.' Harold's nose was in the air.

'Where's Whit-field?' no wonder it took Keeley Brimstone so long to do her job.

'Whit-field is just up the road, between Radcliffe and Prestwich.'

'Oh, you mean *Whitefield*' Keeley was getting to the end of her tether with Harold.

'NO. IT'S *WHIT-FIELD*!' Harold insisted.

'If you raise your voice at me again, *sir,* I will have to call security.'

'I did not raise my voice' Harold sort of angrily whispered. 'I *AM* homeless, and I am being forced to move to Whit-field. My sister pretended to be me and has signed my name for me!' Harold leaned forwards over Keeley Brimstone's desk. He was so close that she could smell the awful pungent, unidentifiable aroma that is Harold. Keeley's mouth turned into an upside-down frown. Her nose crinkled in disagreement.

'What's that smell? Can you smell... err it smells like off fruit... or something...'

'I can't smell anything' he sniffed. 'But I am homeless' Harold sat back in the benefits centre's chair.

'Hang on, your sister signed for you? On your behalf? So you made yourself homeless?'

'No, she signed my name, without my consent!'

'No, that is not how it works, Mr Goatshed' Keeley had to double-check the application form before saying his name. 'Your sister would not have been able to sign for you; it would have to be witnessed. You must have signed it. As so, you have made yourself homeless.'

'You just said I wasn't homeless.'

'You have put yourself in this situation' Keeley blinked away Harold's flippancy. 'You only have yourself to blame. I can't help you... NEXT!' she shouted towards today's queue of destitute of Radcliffe.

'Fill one of the forms in from over there' a toothless man with long hair pointed Harold in the right direction for an application for re-housing 'Get your name on the list anyhow.'

Harold picked up the form. Forms, queues, and waiting lists. None of this would have happened if it wasn't for Sharon. I mean, Shania. And where was she? In a queue to board a plane to Australia most likely. Harold thought about trying to sue her and her solicitors, who had believed her story. But Harold was so dodgy that he decided against getting wound up in litigation. Harold hoped Shania had neglected to wear flight socks and would grow herself a thrombosis on the flight. During the walk home in dog shit valley, I mean Radcliffe, Harold mulled things over. Keeley Brimstone's phraseology 'roofless' got him thinking; roofless sounds like 'ruthless' and that was what Harold needed to do. He would not be handing the keys over to Lenny and Morgan.

Harold would formulate a protest, he would adopt all kinds of dirty tricks. (He decided against a dirty protest in the true sense of the phrase. Not because of the smell. Harold already smelled, but he was

constipated). He would even get into the loft and do a roof protest if needed. Harold loved getting his name in the local newspaper. This time, he was aiming for local news reports, on television if he could manage it. Harold planned
to get himself on *Granada Reports* with his unfortunate predicament. Then it would go viral, and then Sharon/Shania would get to hear about it. Then she would be exposed as the internet bully who manipulated her boyfriend Kevin's wife. Oh, I might be getting ahead of myself here. It's Harold's fault. The outcome Harold was hoping for was to be able to stay put. That is all he was asking, to stay put in Radcliffe. (Although, becoming famous was an added incentive).

Chapter 14: Casanova.

It had been raining for days on end. A 'STORM', they had said so on the news. A disturbed state of the astronomical body's atmosphere. Wind, hail, rain, and a rabbit's hutch blown away in Brandlesholme. A cyclone in Whitefield! The endless storms had caused severe disruption across the U.K. Flooding, pubs destroyed, power cuts in Radcliffe. Flags cracked by lightning outside Curmudgeon Avenue, and today Edith had a dentist appointment.

When she was a young woman, Edith romanticised about a suitor sweeping her off her feet, she dreamt he would surprise her with a surging whirlwind of love. This tall, charming Casanova would knock at her parent's front door, for no other reason than to single Edith out and rescue her from her perceived confines.

'Edith, I know we have never met, but I'm gorgeous, how about it, Love?'

Edith fantasised about this hero taking her as his wife, and loving her so much that he would spend all his money on her. Just enough to keep her in fancy clothes, (Edith would not be greedy). In this imagined life, she would never have to work, and would never, ever have to step into a deceptively deep puddle, as she had on this weather-weary morning.

This puddle had immersed Edith's right leg in rainwater up to her knee. Reminding her of the imaginary hero, who had never materialised. Reg had appeared instead, and she had given birth to her son, Ricky Ricketts. Reg eventually died of a massive heart attack, as you know. And in any case, Edith had worked for her money (which had never been for clothes or fancy footwear). Now, Ricky Ricketts was continually asking for handouts of that money. Not to mention Curmudgeon Avenue's repairs that Edith had jointly inherited with her sister. Sighing, Edith looked at the sky. It was the same dark grey of cloud that was hanging over her (no wonder she was day-dreaming of an imaginary husband).

Edith did not want to be late back, but dentist appointments often elongate. It was still raining when she was done. Shutting herself inside the safety of her car, she sped off home, the sun crept out of the grey clouds. Joining a queue of traffic, Edith seemed to be going in the same direction as the waste paper bin lorry. The wind had got up, the and bits of paper blew around the road like confetti. Someone's discarded shopping list landed on her windscreen.

'CORNFLAKES, CIDER, CONDOMS.'

My goodness! What kind of party are they having? Edith read the list but neglected to keep her eyes on the road. She cringed at the thought of her own shopping list escaping from the bin lorry, without confidentiality, for all to see. Note to self, Edith. From now on, shred the shopping list. Incontinence panty liners are your business and your business alone. Oh! This bin lorry is shedding its load in the wind! Edith had no choice but to make a turn and head for the fast lane, rather than follow this death trap. She was not one for motorway driving, but today in a rush and avoidance of recycling left Edith no choice.

By 10.30, the morning congestion (including bin lorry) had drained away. Tarmac shone in front of her like stretched black leather. Edith had no further need for the fast lane; she was leaving at the next junction. The rain had started again. Edith hesitated to turn her windscreen wipers on because she noticed something... A yellow plastic envelope shoved under the left wiper. The same shiny colour of yellow as a child's painting.

'A PARKING TICKET!' Edith's heart thumped in her chest 'This has *never* happened to me before!'

In sheer panic, she turned the windscreen wipers on after all. The new batch of rain was wiped away, along with the yellow plastic envelope, fluttering away on the breeze, lost forever... heading straight for the windscreen of the car behind her. Edith's initial reaction was to pull over and retrieve the parking ticket. Her car now approached the traffic lights at the junction of the motorway turn off. In her panic, she turned the wipers on full pelt, beeped her horn by accident, and stalled the car. Above her, the sky looked like porridge.

Edith jumped out of her skin at a loud knock on her windscreen. A tall, charming Romeo stood next to her car with the yellow plastic envelope in his hand. When Edith wound down the window, she did not recognise him at first. She blamed the weather, although, what kind of woman cannot remember her imaginary husband?

'Well, hello! I think this belongs to you!' he handed her the parking ticket. 'You look a proper little damsel in distress to me!' the man beguiled.

'Thank you' Edith breathed. Yes, she had just thanked the hero for giving her a parking ticket 'I'm Edith' she did not quite catch his name because of the weather, but it sounded like he had said:

'I'm gorgeous. Can I take you for a cuppa? How about it, Love?' like a real storm in a teacup.

Chapter 15: Edna Cannot Bear to Tell Her Nephew That She Cannot Bear Him.

'Mum! Mum! Are you in? You did say you'd be in this morning, I hope you're not wasting my time again!' this was being shouted through my letterbox on Curmudgeon Avenue. Ricky Ricketts had an arrangement with his mother, explaining why Edith had rushed to get home (she had carelessly double-booked). Edith could rely on Edna to entertain Ricky while he waited, Edna could not stand her nephew. She never liked him as a child, and she certainly had not taken to him as an adult. But Edith, ever forgiving continued to spoil and give in to Ricky's demands, convincing herself it was a mother's duty. (Although it was rather unfortunate that her son was not very likeable). After plenty of racket and rattling of the brass door knocker, Edna answered the front door to Ricky Ricketts against her better judgement.

'Arrite' Ricky said as he shoved himself past his aunt, who was by no means used to being shoved about. He smelled of cigarettes, stolen aftershave and leather jackets. Edna smelled of her own musty existence and disgust.

'Hello, your mother's not in at the moment, gone to the dentist but I'm sure she said it wouldn't take long.' Edna looked out of the kitchen window and spotted a single magpie right in her line of vision. Ricky Ricketts had followed her all the way to the kitchen from the front door with the same surly unblinking expression on his ugly face. 'Is it still three sugars in your tea?' Edna said.

'Yeah,' he sulked, looking away, hopefully at that

same single magpie that Edna had just spotted.
Dragging his booted feet into the living room, Ricky
threw himself onto the leatherette settee. He put his
feet on the chair arm, knocking his mother's library
book onto the floor. Relieving it of its bookmark and
leaving it facedown with the pages splayed out like a
bent fan. (Animal!) He pushed out his lips into a
rubbery oblong shape and breathed out an entitled
sigh. Edna felt obliged to sit with him in the living
room, obliged and protective against potential
pilfering.

'I said I would come round to check on you two,
there has been a lot of people like you taken
advantage of around here.' when Ricky Ricketts
spoke, he displayed brown, rectangular-shaped teeth.
The type of teeth that always made Edna think her
nephew was a criminal, or a conman at least, the very
kind of person he was trying to warn her against.

'People like *me*?'

'Yeah, old ladies. My girlfriend's mum, Patchouli,
has had to be put on a guardianship order, for her own
safety. Wantha makes all her decisions for her after
what happened to her.' Ricky Ricketts sat up, making
the leatherette settee squeak, and the living room
stench of his smell. 'It's something you and mum want
to think about.'

'Well, I usually make all the decisions.' Edna was,
of course, affronted. Then she thought about her sister
wheedling around the kitchen choosing Edna's last
twenty or so meals. Therefore Edith made most of the
decisions at Curmudgeon Avenue (not Edna).

'No' Ricky Ricketts sat forwards with his hands
clasped on his lap 'I'm talking about for both of you. I
could be in charge of it all for you, I don't mind.'

'Well, I do.' Edna blurted out. Ricky Ricketts slanted his eyebrow at her in suggested threat. 'I'm quite capable thank you!'

'Well, I'm just saying there have been a lot of conmen in the area, taking advantage. You want to be careful who you open the door to.'

Yes, Ricky Ricketts had a point; it was a great shame that Edna had opened the door to him. Now, where was Edith?

'I think I should move in here, I know you've got a room going spare' he said, looking up towards the ceiling as though he was taking in a cabinet of curiosities.

'Well, we have to rent that out, we need the money for a new roof!' Edna said, instantly regretting sharing personal information with Ricky. 'Who told you that anyway?'

'Oh, it's all over social media, about men pretending to be interested in romance then stealing all your money.'

'No, I meant how did you know we have a room up for rent? You couldn't have seen the advert in Mrs Ali's shop, she's banned you hasn't she?'

'That was a misunderstanding, and it was Wantha, my girlfriend who told me.'

'Oh, that young... woman? She gave the impression she wanted nothing more to do with you!' Edna pursed her lips.

'Another misunderstanding.' Ricky Ricketts batted his aunt's questioning away. 'Anyway, what's this about a roof? Let me get my man in, he'll sort it out, he owes me... mates rates.'

'No... No thank you, we have a roofer.' Edna was quick off the mark because Ricky Ricketts was offering gifts Edna did not want.

'Yes, but I'm trying to solve your problem here if you'll listen to me.'

Here it comes, Ricky Ricketts, master manipulator.

'Harry the Bastard will fix your roof for free because he owes me, then you won't need the money, then I can move in because I'm family. Also, I can protect you from these conmen.'

'Watch your language around me thank you, this is *Whitefield* you're in, you know.'

'Whitefield! Pah! Anyway, what do you mean language? Ohhh, do you mean Harry the Bastard?' Ricky Ricketts put his best condescending head shake on for his aunt. 'He's not really a bastard, just a big *Game of Thrones* fan. Do you know what that is? It's an epic novel series which has been made into a best-selling drama.'

Edna did not know what to say, her nephew had cornered her, with promises of cowboy roofers allegedly named after literature, in the living room with the leatherette settee and the silver rose vase kept for collecting paper poppies in. But he hadn't finished yet.

'Of course, I can't expect you and Mum to look after me, I mean my grandparents were only *my grandparents*. I can't expect to be entitled to inherit their big, four-storey house, can I? I'm only their only grandson. Unless you are counting Matteo, your lesbian's adopted son? Did he get anything Auntie?'

What a horrible little twerp Ricky Ricketts is. Edna was fuming, but what could she say? Matteo had landed Edna in financial difficulty and robbed her of her longstanding romance with his mother, Genevieve Dubois. Edna could not bear to tell her nephew that she could not bear him.

'What's up, cat got your tongue?' Ricky Ricketts said, (I told you he is a horrible little twerp).

Just then, Edith arrived home, entering the scene on this day of disruptive weather. Late by at least an hour but not because of fillings or root canals. And she was about to prove her horrible son's safeguarding theory.

'This is Maurice!' Edith announced, pink-faced with introductions of a Casanova wearing a raincoat, a turquoise tank-top – and of all things, a cowboy hat… I ask you- who wears a cowboy hat in Whitefield?!

Samantha Henthorn

Chapter 16: Sibling Rivalry.

Edna and Maurice recognised one another instantly, but neither wished to admit to it. They had become acquainted many decades ago when Edna, at the encouragement of their neighbour Madame Genevieve Dubois entered the world of local artists. At the time, Maurice was the aficionado of a local art group in the Methodist Church Hall on the main road.

That period in Edna's life had been kind to her appearance. Massive plastic sunglasses in a variety of colours (usually black). Flowered full-length dresses in polyester, typically black, sometimes see-through (but not on purpose). It had been the hottest summer on record the year when Edna's life changed. And here was Maurice, turning up at Curmudgeon Avenue like a bad penny. Edna had not seen Maurice since she started calling herself an artist, and dumped him unceremoniously when she fell in love with Genevieve. This, I must insist is a story for a later date...

I forgot to mention, Edna dated Maurice, now here he was in Curmudgeon Avenue. Charming her sister like a pink-faced teenager, wearing the same old turquoise tank top. (His purple flares had been abandoned). Edna had been fascinated with his hair back in the day, mustard coloured using a tint designed for women. This experiment in colour now faded apart from the twinkle in his eye - the twinkle of a conman.

'We've just been out to a café. Oh, hello Ricky.' Edith fawned apologetically at her son. The two latecomers stood in the hall just outside the front room, not daring to enter the den that in the last few seconds had unexpectedly allied Edna to her nephew.

'Out... to a café?' Ricky spat. 'You were meant to be meeting me here, you know.'

'Oh.' entered Maurice. 'Having another cash-flow problem, are you? Your mother told me all about it.'

Edna and Ricky gasped in unison. 'Who are you, old man?' and 'Mind your own business, Maurice, how could you, Edith?!' they screamed at the same time.

'OH' blushed Edith, flummoxed by the reaction her imaginary husband had on her sister and son. She smelt jealousy on Edna, a cross she had carried all her life. It was not Edith's fault that Edna was jealous of her. And as for Ricky, floods of Maurice promising to stand up to her son swam around Edith's mind when Maurice spoke the words *'cash-flow problem'*. If Edith was not already enamoured by Maurice, she was now.

There ensued awkward mumblings of *'Would you like another cup of tea?'* and *'No, I'll have to use your toilet if I do!'* Followed by scoffs of disgust from Edna.

'See you on Sunday, my little damsel in distress!' Maurice took Edith by the hand and kissed her knuckles before bowing and leaving Curmudgeon Avenue.

Edith had but a few seconds to enjoy the first flush of love she felt for Maurice. Those few seconds were long enough for Edith to dream up a fantastical life for herself and her imaginary husband. No longer imaginary - Maurice was real, and he had saved her today from the perils of a lost parking ticket. The perils of a life without an imaginary husband who would stand by her side and protect her from her own money-grabbing son. It only took Edith a few seconds to get carried away. These few seconds lasted longer than was reasonably necessary, she had her back turned on her sister and son, and started to look like there was something wrong with her. Edna could not bear standing next to her nephew the smell of cigarettes, and stolen cologne was strong, and so she was the one who broke the silence.

'Edith, how did it go at the dentist?'

'Never mind that!' Ricky Ricketts interrupted, the smell of his brown teeth diffused the hallway. 'He is exactly the kind of con-merchant I was just telling my Auntie Edna about!'

Despite her disgust, Edna felt a very slight twinge of warmth towards Ricky Ricketts when he referred to her as *'My Auntie'*. Nevertheless, she was stuck between a rock and a hard place here. Go along with her nephew's plan to have their assets frozen in a capacity battle, *or* encourage her sister's romance with Maurice the artist? (Who Edna had unceremoniously dumped all those years ago). Edna's pause had also lasted too long, long enough for Ricky Ricketts to conclude that he had been right all along about the two women requiring help.

'I got a parking ticket!' Edith blurted out, she then went on to tell Edna all about it, the puddle, the parking ticket, the cup of tea. Edith could not stop talking. While all this was going on, Ricky Ricketts had just long enough to consider his options. Maybe his mother and auntie genuinely did need someone to look after them. His mother was appearing to be gradually smaller; his auntie had just been staring into space. These, considered Ricky Ricketts were the first signs of old age. Now his mother and auntie huddled in the cupboard under the stairs whispering about something. And what of this Maurice chap? *See you on Sunday?* The thought of his mother dating made him shudder. But worse, the idea of having to look after her made him nauseous. His woman, Wantha, was practically attached to her mother Patchouli - all because she left the hob on overnight! And those carer payments are just not worth it. No. Ricky Ricketts had considered his options and reached a conclusion.

'Right, I'd better get off, I've got ... y' know stuff to do.' Ricky flapped his greasy leather coat shut and exited Curmudgeon Avenue the way he had come in. Edna and Edith momentarily stopped chattering and watched him leave.

'I thought you needed to borrow some more money?' Edith shouted after her son.

'Shh, no leave him to it, Edith' said Edna 'Anyway, I'm getting to what I need to tell you about Maurice.'

Edna went on to warn Edith against any entanglements with the cowboy hat-wearing Casanova. His questionable sexuality, his abstract expressionist action-painting that involved nudity in the Methodist Church Hall. And worst of all for Edna, send Maurice to the bar with a twenty-pound-note, and you would never get any change. Or was that Harold she was remembering? (Shudder).

'Oh, I'm not stupid, Edna! You're jealous! I remember you leaving that painting group in Prestwich, and it had nothing to do with a love triangle! It was all over that vicar being a vegetarian and the complaints about the nude models for the life drawing!'

'Jealous? Me? Of you? Ha! Don't be ridiculous,

Edith, why on earth would I be jealous of you? I just -
don't you think it's a little strange? Going out with a
man your sister has been out with?'

Edith remembered a private thought about Harold,
another male she had coveted from Edna. That's twice
in one day Harold had popped up. Enough to make
Curmudgeon Avenue's toes curl and pavements crack.

Samantha Henthorn

Chapter 17: After Eight on a Sunday.

Edna glanced through the frosted glass in the front
door. The smokiest plum of dusk was highlighted by
the streetlamps and reflected by a shiny silver
moustache, being preened in the reflection of the
window pane. This facial brush belonged to Maurice.
Edna's gaze followed the contours of his face and met
his beady eyes, shaded by matching silver eyebrows,
now wiggling at her. Tap-tap... tap. He sarcastically
abused the brass door knocker. Begrudgingly, Edna
opened the door, and in an involuntary and self-
shaming impulse, her mouth started watering as her
eyes were drawn to the contents of Maurice's right
hand. Long, sleek, dark, mouth-watering sickly sweet
minty chocolate treats.

'Oh, I love those! Edna, do you remember? You
used to batter me for nicking the wrappers!' Edith
bounded down the stairs like a puppy, pushing Edna
out of the way to greet Maurice.

'Actually, Edith I've brought these for your sister. I
do believe they are Edna's favourites, she was always
craving mints... and chocolates.' Maurice tipped his
cowboy hat, nodding towards Edna, whose hands
accidentally reached for the rectangular box of after-
dinner chocolate mints.

(First of all, who wears a cowboy hat in Whitefield?
And second, was Maurice going to admit previous
relations with Edna to her sister Edith? Perfumed and
anticipating a Sunday night date?)

'And I brought these for you,' Maurice reached
inside his tweed blazer for a bunch of supermarket
roses. He managed to uncover the bouquet without
catching any thorns on his turquoise tank top.

'Oh thank you, Maurice!' Edith blushed, a mannerism she had not enjoyed for quite some time. Edna watched through the net curtains as Edith stepped into Maurice's kingfisher blue Triumph Acclaim. She popped one *After Eight* mint in her mouth after the other.

'I thought we'd try that new artisan place on the corner of the main road, they have a gin bible you know Edith, my apologies, you do like gin don't you? Or are you more of a Prosecco girl? That's what all the ladies are drinking these days...' Maurice painted a fancy lifestyle in just a few words.

Edith became drunk and hiccupping after just a few gulps of fashionable Italian sparkling wine. Unfortunately, this meant that Maurice got to find out all about Edith's financial difficulties, the hole in her roof and the loss of her parents at the hands (feet actually) of a fugitive elephant. Maurice listened with feigned interest. Edith's initial disclosure of her adult son pilfering all her money had led Maurice to believe that she had plenty. Still, the four-storey house in a sought after location... (Curmudgeon Avenue? This line of intention is enough to make anyone's Victorian plumbing fail). But this was not why Maurice was really here... As the date continued, Edith could not stop talking. Maurice was treated to further details of Edith's plans for the future. Intentions to restart her diet because last time it didn't work... Every new story always led back to Edith, she loved talking about herself, each sentence starting with *'so anyway'*.

Now Maurice was bored out of his mind, but in amongst all Edith's detail, he did take note of one crucial piece of information:

EDITH GOES OUT WITHOUT HER SISTER EVERY SECOND WEDNESDAY TO KNITTING CLUB.

Maurice could not believe his luck; here he had accidentally bumped into Edna's boring sister after stalking the pair for quite some time. And now he had the chance to exact his revenge on the woman, the bitch who dumped him, unceremoniously and robbed him of his artistic talent. That's right, not only was Maurice the type of conman that Ricky Ricketts had warned against; He had spent the last few decades blaming Edna Payne for his inadequate art adventures. Edna was for the chop. Here we have a potential murder mystery, and let me tell you, this kind of thing has never happened on Curmudgeon Avenue before.

'So anyway I did try knitting underwear, but it didn't work.' *Oh no!* Edith started giggling and trying to look sexy. The mention of underwear, the little pause and 'hmm' sound made to intonate flirtation. Maurice felt a little queasy, but, remembering his cause had to put up with it. Even when he dropped Edith off, the smell of damp floral flannelette up his nostrils almost put him off. Edith's kiss-shaped fuchsia lips and closed eyes afforded Maurice the chance to glance up towards the windows of Number One Curmudgeon Avenue. Ancient net curtains twitched, and he knew, he knew then that it would only be a matter of time.

'Well... hmm... there it is, so ... I think you're a nice lad and hmmm... I owe you a drink... hmm...' Edith giggled and flirted her soul out right there at the front door her head wobbled in unfounded conceit. Her heart in her thermals, Maurice *is* her imaginary husband, don't forget. He tipped the brim of his cowboy hat (who on earth wears cowboy hats in Whitefield?) And wished Edith goodnight.

The following Sunday, Edith waited patiently in the vestibule for Maurice. Edna breezed past her in chiffon. 'Do you think Maurice meant this Sunday or next Sunday?' younger sister pleaded.

'Ha! He's probably changed his mind after seeing me. I told you he fancied me.' Edna said while looking down her nose at Edith. But just as she swept her shawls away into the front room (*Countryfile* was just about to start), the noise of the brass knocker erupted through the hallway.

'Maurice!' Edith squealed, and off she went into Whitefield's Sunday evening, making a show of herself again with Italian sparkling wine.

Well, Maurice's kingfisher blue Triumph Acclaim rolled up and down Curmudgeon Avenue several times over the next few weeks. Each time, a box of *After Eight* mints were foisted upon a wary, but accepting Edna. Each time, Edith fell just that little bit more in lust with Maurice. Each time, his turquoise tank top got a little more plucked by the supermarket roses. But he needn't worry, Edith was so in love, she had prematurely started to show her affection by knitting Maurice a new tank top. Initially, this was a secret tank top. Only the members of the knitting club knew of its existence. Joyce, Edith's friend, had offered to keep it in her knitting hold-all so that even Edna did know out about it.

Such privacy was not required, however. Edna did not give a shit, and Maurice never got past the vestibule when collecting Edith for their Sunday night frivolity. But Joyce and the other knitters need not know this. Edith had shared a little of her imagination with them and had moved Maurice into their fantastical life together. The knitting club will never know that this was all bullshit!

Meanwhile, back at Curmudgeon Avenue, Maurice tried to re-acquaint with Edna. He turned up at Mrs Ali's shop and bought his usual supplies of dinner mints and anti-freeze.

'If you don't mind me saying, why do you need antifreeze at this time of year?' Mrs Ali is naturally nosy as you know and had become increasingly curious about the cowboy wearing mustachio man. 'Only... I only stock it after that bad winter we had a few years ago, this street was gridlocked because of all the frozen vehicles!'

Maurice did not answer. He should have been more careful, he should have found an alternative supplier for his murder weapon. Maurice was a fledgeling criminal, he had got the idea from the television, he did not know how long it would take, and it was already too long. Edith, his proposed victim's sister, was already talking about overnight stays, holidays and birthday presents. Maurice rattled the brass knocker and waited for Edna to answer.

Edna was upstairs in the loft conversion, the room that needed roof repairs. Alone with her thoughts, desires and memories. The re-appearance of Maurice, (the experiment in colour) had brought back the past for Edna. The painting group, and the day that Edna's sophisticated French neighbour stood smoking at her front door. Edna had forgotten her key, Mme Dubois invited her in. Following her up the stairs, Edna explained the whole sorry story about her best piece of art being ruined. Her charcoal life drawing rained off the canvas, nipples and all. Madame Dubois spoke so succinctly, with beauty in her French accent, (which allowed her to speak her mind without insulting her guest). This had been the first day that Edna felt she knew Mme Dubois well enough to address her by her first name: *Genevieve*. This was also the first time that Edna had entered Genevieve's front room. Dove grey blinds, silk-screened wallpaper with a Chinoiserie bird pattern. A white Damask couch that was shaped in such a way squint your eyes, and it could be a Chaise Longue.

'Your front room is lovely!' Edna had cooed. There was nothing more sophisticated than a French neighbour at the time. Edna remembered the two coffee cups on the glass-topped table. Where Edna *imagined* herself as sophisticated, Genevieve had no need to imagine. And with Genevieve's repeated *'Ca Va's'* that was that. It had been a hot June day, with showers and sun shining through the blinds. The two women looked at each other, and without warning, they started snogging each other's faces off right there on the couch. Genevieve glamorous, like a bottle of French perfume. Edna ordinary, like a half-used bottle of bubble bath… Matteo, home from school, arriving at the top of the stairs just at that moment, like a scene from a classic French farce.

'Qu'est-ce que c'est?' he had said.

Ahh, the past! A cruel mistress, Edna. Shame your memories of Madame Genevieve Dubois don't materialise her. Instead, you must endure Maurice, who has fallen in love with your sister, Edith... or has he? Mwah haha!

Chapter 18: Maurice and Edna.

'Knock, knock, knock' the front door rattled Edna out of her memories. Maurice was persistent with that door knocker, like watching a horror movie before bedtime. The second Wednesday had grown to be Edna's alone time since the two sisters were reunited in habitude. For the last three weeks, however, there had been a knock at the door, followed by strange exchanges of after-dinner mints by a man who would not take no for an answer. Edna argued with herself that she did not want to be rude by rejecting Maurice's attempts at re-acquaintance. Still, if she had been frank with herself, a gift of chocolates every other week was the real reason for opening the door. The possibility of hurting her sister's feelings a mere side issue.

Edith had always been the most sickeningly charming of the two sisters. Fat, fair and sweet like a kitten or a day old lamb - that sort of attractive. Edna, refusing to accept this had created a distinct look for herself involving an abundance of expensive makeup and clothes. Before long, Edith had been considered the ugly sister, not Edna. These rivalling tactics were second nature to Edna, and this is why she found herself reaching out and accepting yet another box of *After Eight* mints.

'Maurice!' Edna dismissed. 'Chocolates? Already opened?'

'Oh! I thought you had arthritis! I was just trying to help...' Maurice blurted out his prepared reason for the missing cellophane wrapper. Edna, of course, was affronted.

'Arthritis? Err no... I thought you'd been helping

yourself on the way here!' Edna's voice sounding even posher, and her tone accusatory. (Why don't you buy your own chocolates, Edna?)

Receiving a gift of chocolate mints is almost the same as watching your favourite film when it comes on the television at Christmas - even though you have the DVD. Edna was keeping her enemy close here, hypersensitive to the threat of conmen knocking on the door, after Ricky Ricketts' report. Her vanity was also getting the better of her. To Ricky Ricketts, Maurice may be chatting up the two sisters so he could steal off them, but *obviously* (to Edna) he *wanted her body...* Here it comes...

'Edna...I don't see any point in you being lonely on a Wednesday...' Maurice bravely stepped inside the hallway, grabbing Edna by the forearm. He was deeper inside Curmudgeon Avenue than he had ever been permitted. Edna's sturdy wrist and rock-solid ulna bone, (although wrapped in paper-tissue-like skin) braced in indignation at Maurice's advances. She had not been so close to a member of the male species since nineteen eighty-something, and that male may well have been Maurice. 'Edna, are you feeling faint at all?' Maurice was desperate to know the outcome of his murder attempt, but as he squeezed her wrist, Edna's pulse quickened, and her face reddened.

'Faint? Do I look like the sort of person who would feel faint?' Edna, as you know, does not suffer fools gladly.

'No, it's just this time of year, and so on... I thought you looked a bit worried, I was just making conversation really.' Maurice, the fledgeling murderer, now cowered in the corner of the vestibule, returning to his original permitted place. When he was alone at home, (wearing his cowboy hat), Maurice had imagined a violent and bloody end for Edna, including swear words and spilt guts. Maurice had imagined returning home and immediately regaining his imagined talents in the field of artwork. He painted murder scenes - Edna's end. His imaginings took him as far as the Portico library in Manchester, the Tate Gallery in London. (But dismissed the Louvre on account of his dislike for the channel tunnel). Maurice was enjoying his imagined fantasy about a BBC4 documentary based on his life in partnership with the Open University; when he realised he was now on the floor of Curmudgeon Avenue's vestibule.

'Oh not you as well. Henri the Third keeled over half an hour ago, he's been feeling queer for the past few weeks.' Edna resisted the urge to kick Maurice in the thigh. 'Are you alright, Maurice?' she huffed, don't forget he had been hampering Edna's alone time.

'Oh, yes, I must apologise.' Maurice dabbed his moustache with a purple handkerchief.

Edna then grabbed him by both hands in order to pull him up to his feet, and hopefully end this awkward and unnecessary rendezvous. They stood there in the hallway, holding hands. 'Who is Henri the Third?'

'He's my cat, of course, I must tell you he is the one with after-dinner mints as favourite! I've never known a cat like him!'

Maurice's eyes widened. 'Your cat has been eating the chocolates?'

'Oh, don't chastise me, he has always had a sweet tooth. I've been trying to perk him up, he seems very listless at the moment. I know it's unorthodox, but I thought a few of these mint chocolates might be just the trick.'

Maurice and Edna faced one another, still holding hands.

'At first, they seem to be working, he perked up! Couldn't get enough of them! But then he seems to go floppy for the rest of the afternoon.' Edna now felt that she and Maurice had been holding hands for longer than was reasonably necessary. And Maurice's virility had also flopped. They both turned towards the door as an engorged Edith entered the scene. Her face fell flat, however at the sight of Maurice and Edith holding hands.

'I knew it!' Edith's heart broke, right there and then into a thousand pieces 'I saw your car as I was on my way to the knitting group, Maurice, and I wanted to finish my present to you! My knitting! I have knitted this with love for you, Maurice, and here you are canoodling my sister!' Edith emotionally held the newly knitted, Prussian blue tank top in double yarn, each word accompanied by all of Edith's strength and forceful introduction of the crafted item.

'Edith' Maurice said with apathy 'It's not what you think...'

Edith warmed to Maurice's warm tones. She had not wanted to believe anything could happen in this day and age with Maurice and her sister. And she did not wish to accept she could be disappointed in love, especially as she has been knitting a tank top.

'Well, what is it then?' Edna said. You would think that she felt ashamed or saddened by her sister's noticeable heartbreak, not the case. Edna was thinking about herself. Never had she been flushed

out of a flirtation, not since Harold Goatshed took her on a double date with Babycham Barbara. Edna was not about to let this happen again.
(Harold keeps getting a mention, I feel nauseous!) Maurice opened his mouth to speak, but he was interrupted by Curmudgeon Avenue's naturally nosy corner shop proprietor. 'Oh, has your car broken down again?' Mrs Ali addressed Maurice 'I didn't know you were visiting the sisters all these weeks, I would have given you a discount!' Mrs Ali lied.

'The Cortina is working just fine thank you, Mrs Ali.' Edna answered the question intended for Maurice with clipped tones. Only then Edith turned to face their neighbour, she never wore much mascara. Just enough to run down her face like Alice Cooper at the slightest hint of upset.

'Oh! My goodness are you feeling alright, Edith?' Mrs Ali enquired.

'She's fine. She just got her knickers in a twist because Maurice came round to give me a box of mint chocolates'

'Mint chocolates and antifreeze, every other Wednesday afternoon!' Mrs Ali confirmed.

'Yes, quite,' Edna said not entirely understanding the antifreeze bit. Edith was still standing at the front door clutching the hand-knitted (with love) tank top. Maurice decided to leave before the conversation became any more incriminating. He squeezed his way out of Number One Curmudgeon Avenue and put his cowboy hat back on his head.

'Excuse me, ladies.' Edith then let out a small cry, Maurice turned to her 'I'm sorry Edna... I mean, Edith.'

And with further wails of heartbreak from Edith, just like that, Maurice was gone.

Chapter 19: A Lot of it About in Whitefield.

'There's a lot of it about, in Whitefield' the vet said. 'Unfortunately, of course.'
Just like that, Henri the Third had gone. Just as Edna thought he was picking up, he keeled over and breathed his last. The suddenness of the incident made the sisters walk all the way to the vets, despite it being too late. And just as Mrs Ali had predicted, Henri the Third was the victim of poisoning by antifreeze.

'You could report it to the police of course, but it's not for me to say if they will do anything about it.' the vet said.

'I thought you just said there's a lot of it about?'

'Oh Edith, that's just a figure of speech, vets are always saying things like that' Edna patronised her sister, flared her nostrils and turned with purpose to leave. Edith walked away quietly, fastening the rain cape around her neck.

'Erm aren't you forgetting something?' the vet referred to poor Henri the Third's lifeless body on the examining table. Edna looked at Edith and Edith looked at Edna. Then all three looked at the dead cat.

'Well, he's not my cat really...' Edna flicked her hair to one side, Edith started nervously playing with her own. The vet raised an eyebrow.

'Whose cat is he then? I may have to contact the authorities about this myself.'

'Well, he is in my *care* as such,' Edna backtracked. (Don't forget, Henri the Third had initially been Madame Genevieve Dubois' cat, a story I am keen to tell you at a later date.)

'Would you like us to take care of him?' the vet softened her tone.

'Take care of him? He's dead!' Edna said.

'I mean pet cremation. Rossendale pet cemetery are very sympathetic, and you'll be able to collect his ashes, people make little memorials in their gardens.' the vet slid a flyer over to Edna with the detail of cat cremation. It was a shocking amount of money for a sister who was still trying to find the funds for a new roof on a Victorian terrace. Edna thought about how the death of a cat had been dealt with in the past. The original Henri had run away, disappeared '*sooiceed*' Genevieve had pronounced. Henri the second had been run over in the street, Matteo, Genevieve's adopted son, had brought him home ... and had he flushed him down the toilet? Surely not!

'Ms Payne, how would you like us to proceed?' The vet was now conscious of time, there was a Staffordshire bull terrier with the runs in the waiting room.

Edna wrapped her coat and arms around herself, stuck her nose in the air and insisted 'I'm NOT paying!' She wafted through the consulting room doors, smacking Edith in the face. Edith thought better of the arrangement and bundled Henri the Third back into the holdall he had been carried down Manchester road in. 'Thank you doctor' Edith said as she exited the room backwards.

On the way home, they passed the local police station. Edna looked at Edith and Edith looked at Edna...

'Spinster sisters!' cried out the familiar voice of Toonan. (Remember her?) The potential previous tenant was now in cuffs in front of the desk sergeant's glare. 'What are youse doin' in the cop shop?'

'Excuse me, young lady, I'm just about to formally caution you.' the desk sergeant said.

'Alright, keep your hair on' Toonan said to the policeman without fear or respect. 'God they don't half stress in here' Toonan said, turning to Edith and Edna with rolled eyes. 'Let these two old dears go before me if you want.'
I think it might have been the 'old dears' comment that made Edna do it. She shoved Toonan out of the way and emptied Edith's holdall out on the desk. Henri the Third's dead little face flopped out open-mouthed in front of Toonan and her accompanying police officer.

'Eww that's mingin' what did you do that for?' Toonan squirmed.

'I'm distraught Toonan, my cat has been murdered, and I am not moving until something has been done about it!'

It all happened very quickly, shouting, screaming and more shouting. Naturally, Edith was in tears. Edna was manhandled at one point with threats to arrest her for breach of the peace. Eventually, the two sisters and their dead cat agreed to sit in the waiting area of Whitefield Police Station. Crime and first world emergencies happen to the best towns, even Whitefield, and so they had quite a wait on their hands. Toonan, after being 'processed' for some undisclosed crime of the night offered to wait with the two sisters. Then she quickly changed her tune when she discovered they had been travelling on foot, not in the Ford Cortina.

'I'll put the word out in the Frigate' was Toonan's last word. This meant that she would be letting her sister, Wantha and on/off partner Ricky Ricketts know that Henri the Third had been murdered. If only they knew, the intended victim had been Edna.... If only *all* of them knew!

Chapter 20: L'odour du Harold.

'I don't think you've got any choice, it's your house, after all. You two have got no choice but to get the bailiffs in!' Trisha was a general *'know it all'*. She often watched 'documentaries' on the subject when getting ready for her next shift at the Bridge Tavern in Radcliffe.

'Thanks, Trish. Oh, by the way, that girl I was telling you about - dating an older man? Turned out to be the girl's estranged dad!' Lenny was a general gossip on all things Radcliffe. He read 'news' on the subject of life in the North Manchester town at work, in readiness for his daily pint.

Meanwhile, Harold had taken up residence in the loft of his mother's old house. He had even staged a roof-top protest, but no one had noticed. Failing to attract the local press and public, Harold had reached stalemate up there in the loft with a bucket, kettle and supply of dehydrated snacks. He could, and had made one Pot Noodle last all day. Lenny and Morgan had tried to coax Harold down, wafting the smell of bacon up through the loft hatch, but this had little effect on Harold. He pretended to be vegetarian, then he pretended not to care. Then he diffused his own smell down the loft hatch for Lenny and Morgan's consumption. The couple tried not to breathe in the scent of Harold, there was no pretending - it was awful.

While Lenny and Morgan slept, Harold listened out for their snoring, then crept down the loft ladder to attend to his ablutions. And come the morning, Lenny and Morgan would be affronted by the smell of Harold in their bathroom. The bathroom that they so desperately wanted to replace. But this would mean temporarily moving to Morgan's mother's house in Bury. Morgan's mother had a pile of beach towels ready for such an occasion. Still, for Lenny and Morgan, this would have meant leaving their home in Radcliffe unattended, thus allowing Harold to change the locks and perfect his squat. Because that's what it was now, a squat.

Lenny and Morgan had no choice but to put all of their bathroom funds into employing the correct and proper legal strategy to get their unwanted flatmate out. It is an extremely tiresome process for a house to go through, enough to make one's front bedroom windows glaze over. The day had come, the day that the bailiffs were to attend Bronte Crescent in Radcliffe. This sounds a lot more romantic than it was, trust me.

'Hello! Hello Mr Goatshed! Are you there? High court enforcement officers, Sir! Are you going to answer Sir?' the bailiff repeated his tiresome mantra through the letterbox. This type of thing would never happen over in Curmudgeon Avenue, believe me... The chief bailiff had sent his heavyweight sidekick around the back, in case Harold tried to leg it. Although trying to flush him out, a correct and proper legal strategy had to be adhered to, an incredibly boring process for a bailiff.

'There's no movement at the back,' reported the sidekick 'I climbed up on the wall, and I saw him, he's up in the loft.'

Oh crikey, Harold was still up in the loft. Despite his advancing age, he had no problem hearing the bailiff shouting instructions to answer the door. All that time spent up there with a portable television and Freeview box. There was nowt else for him to do but watch daytime TV, the same documentaries about household evictions that Trish from The Bridge had been watching. But which diversion strategy would Harold employ? He stood in the loft space, stooping over with grumblings of entitlement, rolling a ball between his thumb and forefinger. Who did Sharon think she was wading in after all those years, taking over (and paying for) mother's funeral? For-Sale signs up on the two up two down before the ink on the sympathy card had dried? (This was not the case, of course. Sharon had been very patient with Harold). Well, as patient as a person could reasonably be expected to be with a brother like Harold. He was still rolling that ball and would have continued to grumble on to himself, had he not realised that the ball was one of his own turds. Curled up and dry like an out of date Brazil nut, absentmindedly picked from Harold's late-night emergency plastic-bag-toilet up there in the loft space. Filled with rage, he peeped out of a missing slate, at Radcliffe's skyline, it was the colour of dirty dishwater. Harold took aim and threw the turd at the sidekick bailiff stationed in the back yard. He could not even perform a dirty protest properly. It rolled down the remaining roof and landed in the gutter. More undeserved punishment for Lenny and Morgan.

'We're coming in Mr Goatshed!' the chief bailiff and his sidekick gained entry with the front door key given to them by their temporary employers and rightful owners of the house. Harold's house slippers could not gain purchase on the loft ladder quickly enough to barricade the front door.

'Excuse me! What do you think you're doing barging in here?' Harold barked, all red-faced and impudent.

'High court enforcement officers, Sir. We have all the paperwork here to evict you today from this property.' the chief bailiff went on to explain the correct and proper legal proceedings. Lenny and Morgan had paid handsomely, and so it was all above board.

'This is my house! Half of it is my house! My sister had no right to sell it! And for the last six months, I've only been living in a quarter of it!' Harold protested about his sister changing her name from Sharon to Shania. Managing to persuade and manipulate the sale of their mother's house and so on. He did not mention being in fear of reproach for an outstanding motoring offence and his accumulated debt and benefit fraud that would cancel out any ownership. This was a very dull conversation for the bailiff to listen to. He had heard it all before, of course. It wasn't until Harold said 'Look! Look! I haven't even been able to use the facilities!' poking his shit covered fingers towards the bailiff's face, they both had a proper look at each other. 'Hey! I recognise you!' Harold said.

'Yeah, and I recognise you!' the bailiff's sidekick stepped forwards. 'It's him from the Bridge!'

And that's when things took even more of a turn for the worse for Harold. The bailiffs were only Sleeveless Steve and Psycho Steve from The Bridge Tavern, the most popular pub in Radcliffe! Harold was outraged! These two ruffians could not and should not possibly be in such a responsible position!

'I want to see some ID!' Harold folded his arms

like a haughty old woman. The two Steve's produced their ID, nicknames, of course, were not included. These were examined by a clueless Harold, then the three were at a stalemate. Harold opened his mouth to demand further protestations, but he was silenced by Sleeveless Steve. Skilled in the repetition of his memorised speech; Steve allowed Harold one hour to collect his belongings and leave the house he had grown up in. Right there on Bronte Crescent, Radcliffe. The romantic address Harold had swooned many unwilling sweethearts at, in his youth. The address he had returned to as a fully grown middle-aged man when even his mother did not want him. His whole life was bundled into plastic bin liners (sparing the emergency commode bag) and slung into the back of a taxi, followed by Harold.

For months and years to come, especially on that one hot Tuesday morning-per-summer in Radcliffe, guests and passers-by would exclaim *'Why? What's that smell?'* When getting too close to Lenny and Morgan's house. The smell of course had been left behind by Harold, L'odour du Harold.
But for now, he was in a taxi, hurriedly scraping-out loose change from his trouser pockets.

'Where to Mr?' the taxi driver asked.

'Err how far will a fiver get me?'

'Five quid? That'll only get you to Whitefield from here!'
The taxi driver was right. As he rolled up alongside Curmudgeon Avenue, the meter read exactly five pounds.

Chapter 21: Harold Tries to Make a Move.

'Curmudgeon Avenue.' Harold said to himself, smacking his lips together with smug overtones. Harold was sure he had been here before, but it was dark then and several decades ago. Today, the sky was full of curiosity for removal vans and optimism. Harold was ready to put his misfortune behind him and move on. Even if this meant returning to a street that he had walked down once before. Fate had led him there with his five-pound note. Maybe he had taken the wrong turn when he had stepped down Curmudgeon Avenue all those years ago. Maybe, but probably not. Harold was, of course, remembering Edna Payne. Quite a conquest for Harold back in those days, although in the end, he had to admit he had just been using her to try and get Babycham Barbara jealous. And did Edna have a sister? Yes, Harold remembered. She could not stop talking, she was probably still talking right now. However, Harold thought they probably no longer lived in Curmudgeon Avenue. The sister's parents were probably dead, as were Harold's. Time had slipped out of his hands, and the clock was now demanding *'I told you so.'* To this homeless has been, standing under this sky of cobalt and catastrophe. Harold stood stationary, outside Mrs Ali's shop for longer than was reasonably necessary.

'I'm going to start charging you for loitering duties, are you alright, darling?' Mrs Ali stepped out into the sunlight. She thought to herself that it was a shame she did not have a bucket of used mopping up water to swill on the street and this stranger's feet, just like she had seen in the movies.

'Oh, I erm, I used to know someone who lived on

this street I'm just reminiscing.' Harold said to Mrs Ali... and who was she calling 'darling'?

'Really?' Mrs Ali looked Harold up and down. He did not look like your average man from Whitefield, but then who does? Edna and Edith recently had a mystery caller wearing a cowboy hat, with an appetite for antifreeze, so anything goes these days in Curmudgeon Avenue (much to my disgust).

'Yes, the Payne family. Myself and Edna had a bit of a thing a long, loong time ago.' Harold adopted a posh voice, the type he presumed he might find in that part of Whitefield.

'Really?' Mrs Ali was loving this. Every street had to have one of those people who know everyone. This mystery man was not the type of person you might see in the company of Edna Payne, she doubted very much that they had a 'thing'. (Especially not as Edna is a lesbian). Mrs Ali loved this, and she could not resist.

'I don't suppose they still live here? It was their parents' house, of course.' (Harold was one to talk!) 'I heard all these big Victorian terraces have been gutted and turned into apartments.' Harold's neck wobbled like a turkey, and he stroked his chin. His familiarity with Mrs Ali, who had only stepped out of her shop to have a nosy was breeding contempt.

'They do still live there, and no, you're wrong, all the houses in this Avenue are privately owned.' Mrs Ali immediately regretted saying too much, but alas, that is what a busy-body does. Yet, still, she continued to speak: 'They're looking for a lodger, come into my shop - I think I might still have their card.'

And there it was in the window, slightly faded and

curled by the sun like a child's treasure map. The
additional 't' I told you about had faded away,
leaving Edith's original 'Lodger Wanted' plea
reflecting in Harold's spectacles. Fate had blown
Harold Goatshed down Curmudgeon Avenue once
before. If it were not for that taxi driver, safety would
have remained on the avenue.

'I might call on them now, do you know if they're
in?' Mrs Ali had become Harold's go-to in a matter of
a few sentences.

'They've gone out as it goes, Edna's cat died, and
they went to the vet in rather a hurry. They walked
there; between you and me that Cortina of hers has
not seen petrol since January.'

How Mrs Ali knows everything is beyond me. If
Harold had asked what colour dress Edith was
wearing today, she probably would be able to answer.
Goodness! She probably knew what colour
underpants Harold had on right then! Harold left
Curmudgeon Avenue clutching Edna and Edith's
lodger advert. And good riddance to him, although I
despair he will be back, and that is when the fun will
start. Not for me, but for you... Until then, Harold
must go, by foot and announce himself to Keeley
Brimstone at the housing office, he really is homeless
and roofless now. She put him up in the local
Salvation Army Hostel. Just Harold's style. She was
only able to do this because he had convinced her he
was on a promise from Edna… although, I'm relying
on Edna to shun his advances, who in their right mind
would want to house share with Harold? They are still
talking about his rooftop protest in the Bridge Tavern,
Radcliffe to this very day.

It was quite some time before the sisters returned home with Henri the Third (deceased) and they were met by Mrs Ali, who had now perfected that scene from a film she had coveted. 'MRS ALI!' Edna shouted, as the bucket of water met with her leopard print ballet pumps. 'Don't worry, she said by way of engagement 'It's not dirty water, it's that hyacinth disinfectant. I'll give you a discount!'

'Oh Mrs Ali, we haven't had a good day' said Edith. 'Henri the Third died.'

'I know darlings' Mrs Ali said.

'The vet told us to go to the police, then we met the young girl who wanted to move in. She is a *criminal*! Then we had a really long wait, just to report that we thought someone had murdered our cat. They're not going to do anything about it! Just keep it on record!'

'Well, when one door closes, another opens. You've had a visitor while you've been at the... various different locations. He took your lodger card, I think he is looking for a room to rent!' Mrs Ali said.

'A visitor?' the sisters cried out in unison as though Mrs Ali had just told them their house had burned down.

'It wasn't Maurice, was it? The police are looking for him!'

The police were doing no such thing, but Edna could not admit to herself that her day had been wasted.

'He said his name is Harold' Mrs Ali blew a kiss at the sisters and retreated into her corner shop.

'Harold!' they exclaimed in unison again. Edna broke wind silently, her nerves getting the better of her after hearing Harold's name. Edith unlocked the front door of Number One Curmudgeon Avenue.

'You can't blame your farts on Henri the Third anymore, he's dead, Edna.'

Chapter 22: Henri the Third's Funeral.

Edna had not spoken to Madame Genevieve Dubois for about a year, on account of her eventually ignoring Edna's calls. It had all come to a head when Genevieve had a massive argument with her adopted son, Matteo. Genevieve is now a fugitive living somewhere in rural France, allegedly with a new lover. Edna is here, somewhere in Curmudgeon Avenue, heartbroken. Her ex-partner's legal fees are now her legal fees. Mme Genevieve Dubois was always a slippery one...

Edna picked up the telephone. Her mouth was dry, her heart thumped in her strapping ribcage. She has a legitimate reason to contact Genevieve, her cat, Henri the Third has died. Although, Edna found out (by stalking Genevieve on Facebook) that she now has a dog. A *French Poodle* no less, though Edna had been led to believe that Genevieve preferred pussy cats.

The telephone line sang the exotic international dialling tone, Edna almost returned the receiver in fear when the call clicked and was answered.

'Hello,' a distinctly Lancashire lady answered the phone. Edna slammed the phone down in shock. Had she got the wrong number after all? Had Genevieve moved on again? Edna wiped the nervous sweat from her top lip with her turtle neck jumper, while clutching her pearls in the other hand. 'OH!' she cried out in shock as the telephone screamed.

' 'Ello?' a distinctively French accent purred ' 'Ello, oo is this?'

Edna's heart burst, feelings of warm passion radiated within her, her mouth dry with nerves, lips stuck to her teeth.

'Genevieve? Is this you?' Edna said. There was a long pause, then the recipient of the question knew there was no point putting the phone down, she had accidentally spoken to Edna.

'Oh! Oui! I saw thee numbrrr on my caller display, and it looked familiar... Manchester...'

'Yes, Genevieve, I'm living at my parents' house now on Curmudgeon Avenue, it's where we first met, can you believe it?'

'Ah! You have moved without telling me?' Genevieve teased. This time the pause was on Edna's end of the line.

'Well, I thought you didn't want to speak to me. The thing is, Henri the Third has died, so I thought you might want to come to the funeral.'

Both parties were silent on either side of the English Channel. Phone calls like these are expensive, so eventually, Edna blurted out: 'Who answered the phone before?'

'Pardon?' Genevieve said.

'Before, the first time I rang, I thought I had the wrong number?'

'You must be mistaken.'

'No, Genevieve, you said you got this number off the caller display because you ... you know, before when I rang the first time.'

'Non!'

'Yes, Genevieve, whoever *she* was, she sounded very *Mancunian'* Edna did not even want to know, but she was curious.

'Listen, Edna... I will 'ave to let you know about zee funeral' Genevieve changed the subject and her tone to that of a cold day in the Northwest. And with that, she put down the telephone.

Now, pet funerals are not uncommon in the Northwest of England. Usually performed if there is a child in the family, heartbroken and inconsolable at the sudden lesson in mortality that their beloved familiar has provided. Children, on their knees saying a few words of sympathy around a little patch of dug up garden, concealing the corpse of any number of goldfish and hamsters. Henri the Third was due to have a funeral, it seemed the right thing to do. And the most childish person in the house, Edith had decided to write down a few words to say at the ceremony.

'He was a French cat, so he was most likely Catholic...' Edith said to Edna, who was not really listening. 'I know that's a bit of a sweeping generalisation, but well we can't ask him, and I never saw him go to church. He did seem to like fish on a Friday - so that's something to go off.'

'Who are you talking about?' said Edna, (and who are you talking to?)

'Henri the Third, of course!' said Edith.

'He liked to eat fish on *any* day of the week, and of course, he didn't go to church, Edith, he was a cat!' (YOU IDIOT) Edna thought to herself. 'I'm expecting an important telephone call, Edith, and I don't think we should bury him until ... I've had a definite from Genevieve if she is going to attend - he was her cat originally.'

'I thought tuna butties and chocolate mints - he liked those.' Edith said to herself, forgetting that it was the after-dinner delights that killed the cat. Edith's undersized brain then caught up with the conversation 'GENEVIEVE?! Madame Dubois?

Here? On Curmudgeon Avenue, where it all started?'

'Well, nothing's certain, It's of no consequence to me, I just thought I would do the honourable thing and invite her' Edna's nostrils flared, she stuck her nose in the air.

'Oh! We'll have to get the emergency chairs out! I've invited Ricky Ricketts, and he's bringing his on/off girlfriend Wantha, her sister Toonan - depending on if she is in prison or not and their mother, Patchouli. Oh, it's a good job we didn't get a lodger after all!'

'It's only a cat's funeral, Edith!'

'Any reason to get wasted they said.' Edith reported, quite innocently.

Just then, the telephone rang.

'Oh, this will probably be Genevieve!' Edna flushed. She cleared her throat with an air of nonchalance before picking up the receiver 'Yeeeeees' Edna said, in her telephone voice.

'Edna! Is that you? You sound different!' Harold did not sound different, and Edna recognised his voice (both disgusted and disappointedly).

'Who is this?' she lied.

'It's me! Harold! The old dear at the corner shop told me you are looking for a lodger. Look no further, Edna - I'm your man!'

It was a combination of the 'old dear' description of Mrs Ali, (one score younger than Harold at least) - not to mention the shock of hearing his voice all these years later that did it.

'OH! You animal!' Edna play-acted the victim of a funny phone call. 'Do not ring here again... You pervert!' she slammed the phone down and ran upstairs to her attic boudoir.

'Who was it?' Edith asked. It took her the best part of an hour to work out that Edna had been on the receiving end of a telephone sex pest. And even though Edna had been lying, what lay beneath was the ugly realisation that Harold was about to return to Curmudgeon Avenue.

Samantha Henthorn

Chapter 23: The Rarity of Phone Boxes

'Hello,' Harold said.

'Goodbye' Edna slammed the phone down and pretended it was *one of those sales calls.*
Over the past week or so, Edna had attempted to conceal any previous knowledge of Harold. Reason being, she had once made a phone call from a telephone box that had sealed Harold's fate as a petty criminal. The reason he never gave his proper name when he got a new job, (as so often he did) was all Edna's fault. See, she reported an imaginary burglary from one of the many telephone boxes in Whitefield (there were multiple phone-booths in those days). Harold's lowlife reputation was born of Edna's revenge, the origins of which I must insist is a story for a later date. Please do not feel left out - Harold never got to know the identity of his accuser, but I am willing to share what Edna did, all those years ago:

Edna Payne had made a special trip to Stanley Road, far enough from Curmudgeon Avenue (her parent's house at the time); but near enough for her to return home without raising suspicion. On a mission to complete a justifiable crime of revenge against Harold because he dumped her for Babycham Barbara.

'Hello, is that the police?' Edna made her voice quake for added effect.

'Yes, what's your emergency?'

'Well… I've just seen someone… a man climbing over someone's back wall… I think he's a burglar!' Edna had tried hard to conceal her giggles.

'Are you ok love? I know it's a shock to see a crime happen, you're doing well, I have your location but could you give me a description?' the police call handler thought Edna was crying!

'Oh!' fair play to Edna, I don't know how she got her words out between giggles 'He was tall and lanky, he had dark hair... I think I recognised him!'

'Yes? Who is he then? I'll have a patrol car with you as soon as I can.'

'I think... I think it was Harold Goatshed!' Edna managed to blurt out.

'And your name is, please?' the call handler said, (she really should have asked this first). 'Hello? Are you there, Madam?'

But the line was dead. The receiver swung dramatically in the red telephone box, on a Tuesday lunchtime all those years ago. Edna had skipped with joy all the way home, almost wetting herself with laughter at her evil plan, which would change Harold's life. The police had conducted a thorough(ish) door-to-door enquiry of Stanley Road in Whitefield. No burglaries or wall jumpers to report. One young officer, Kevin Legend, got a lead on 'Harold Goatshed'. Having discovered that he drinks in the Bridge Tavern, Radcliffe, enquiries were made there. Harold had an alibi for the date and time of the fictitious crime, he had been trying to sell Maggie Lomax life insurance in her pristine front room. (Minus a dog, on this occasion). Officer Legend's promotion failed to materialise, and Harold was never arrested.

Nevertheless, word got around that Harold had been questioned by police after a mystery female saw him jump into a back garden. Folk gossiped about Harold from the Bridge Tavern in Radcliffe, to the Old Duke in Brandlesholme. As far as the Masons in

Ramsbottom, all the way back to the Frigate in
Whitefield. The story had been whispered so many
times it had changed, resulting in Harold being named
as a 'Peeping Tom' within a ten-mile radius. So you
could sort of understand Harold avoiding the use of
his real name. Edna was unsatisfied with the outcome
of her Tuesday expedition to Stanley Road, she never
got to witness the misery she had caused for Harold.
Edna had no guilt or sympathy about it. Still, you can
sort of understand that she wished to protect herself
from any future reconciliation with such a person.

That is why, during the past week, the telephone
had become her enemy. Harold had been persistent
with those phone calls. For most suburban dwellers,
answering the phone during the day was a somewhat
hazardous affair. You could be minding your own
business, folding laundry or cleaning the bathroom,
when all of a sudden, you are being asked *'How are
you today?'* In a slightly over-familiar fashion. Edna
did not suffer fools gladly, so quickly employed one
of those 'Choose to Refuse' services. Therefore, when
Harold started telephoning, Edith became confused as
to why Edna had started rushing to the phone ... (God
forbid that Edith speak to Harold, we'll never get rid
of him!) And secondly, why the 'sales calls' were
getting through again.

Telephone boxes are few and far between in
modern-day Whitefield; at least one pair of Harold's
shoes were ruined because of fresh urinations on the
floor. (Not belonging to Harold you understand). He
had employed the use of pay-as-you-go SIM cards for
his phone calls to the Payne sisters. Harold, like most
homeless people, changed his phone number
regularly, this afforded him the luxury of getting past

Edna's phone call blocking system. He was determined to live on Curmudgeon Avenue.

'Hello, Edna?' Harold said in understanding tones, he had convinced himself that because women don't usually ignore him, Edna had gone deaf.

'I'm sorry, I can't hear you, don't phone back' Edna had now convinced herself she had heard the last of Harold, after ignoring him all week.

'Hello pet, I hear you have a room for rent, like.' Harold was not very good at accents, he thought this sounded a bit North-East, therefore hiding his own Lancastrian lilt. Edna put the phone down without answering him.

Several more unsolicited phone calls were received by Number One Curmudgeon Avenue. You can imagine how anxious Edna was behind her turtle-neck jumper and flared nostrils. (The methane was mighty in her bedroom). On the seventh day, Harold came up with a brainwave. He would employ the help of his friendly housing officer, Keeley Brimstone.

'I've found somewhere! I've found somewhere to live! It's just that they're not answering the telephone!' Harold had interrupted Keeley's thirty-second lunch break with his announcement, and Keeley was not prepared to celebrate or engage in any housewarming shenanigans. If Harold had found a home, why did he not just go and live there?

'And what, Mr Goatshed do you expect me to do about it?' Keeley said, her granola and yoghurt diet discarded to the left side of her desk.

'Aren't you finishing that? I'll eat it if you don't want it?'

Typical Harold. Keeley did not answer; instead, she asked: 'Have you tried knocking on their door? They may have put the wrong telephone number on their advert.'

'Yes I have, but they're never in, their cat died.' Keeley frowned as she took the dirty piece of paper out of Harold's hand. She dialled the number.

'It's ringing' she rolled her eyes at Harold 'Curmudgeon Avenue? It's nice round there, you'll be lucky to get housed there, Mr Goatshed.' Keeley looked him up and down as the phone rang out. 'I heard they had all got turned into flats, you say this is a room in a house? A shared tenancy?' Just as Keeley was about to put the phone down, Edna answered it, out of breath after running down three flights of stairs.

'Oh, hi, I'm phoning about the room you have for rent, I'm phoning from the housing department. I have a Mr Goatshed here interested in becoming your tenant.' Keeley said, with her telephone voice. Edna broke wind, and it was loud enough for Keeley to hear... It may have been the sound of Harold's name, it may have been nerves at the prospect of having to lie. But Edna was not about to lie, what she was about to say to Keeley was absolutely the truth, even though she had a feeling that Edith would not like it.

'Oh, I'm sorry, I'm afraid the room is taken, I have a tenant due to come round this afternoon' Edna did not say goodbye, she just put the phone down. Breathing out a huge sigh, Edna let rip another loud fart, this one celebratory. That was the end of Harold, or so Edna thought - Edna always thinks she is right, but this time, she was wrong because as you know, Harold is a persistent bugger.

Chapter 24: Georgina Foote, Potential Tenant.

This is the story of how Georgina Foote lost everything. Important, because up until that point, Georgina Foote took *no shit*. She was not your typical nurse, joining the profession late when mature students were encouraged. Her motivation had been a drastic, weird kind of revenge towards her mother, Pauline Foote. You see, it is a well-known fact that social services staff do not get along with NHS professionals. When Georgina first qualified, her mother called her out as a *'typical bloody psychiatric nurse.'* Staff Nurse Georgina strode onto that ward looking old enough to be a ward sister. Jangling the medicine keys, ready to eat patients and student nurses alive. Georgina Foote took no shit. (Although her mother selfishly refused to retire and babysit Georgina's children).

Three children and one husband at home, you would think Georgina had enough on her plate; not the case. Terrible nurses usually do bring the drama. Ask any nurse, they will be keen to tell you about the psychopaths they have had the misfortune of working with. Imagine it, the nurse who is always flouting the uniform policy, neither punctual, polite, nor well presented. The nurse who always requests the *'emergency bank holiday'*. Smoking, drinking (while on duty) and regularly off sick with some excuse. For example, Georgina Foote had not been qualified long when her mother had died *three times*! Each imaginary bereavement landing Georgina with two weeks paid compassionate leave. No one questioned it, with not enough nurses to go around the rota, it would have been difficult to sack her.

It was not, as it turned out difficult to get the sack from her position of common-law-wife to Kevin. This happened in September, where each morning was fragranced with the fresh smell of freedom. Georgina had started *living*. She met Berk during Laura Whale's retirement do at the Turkish Restaurant in Manchester. Berk (his name meant 'man of strength') was working as a waiter that night. Georgina's colleague, Nina, (always up for a giggle) had squeezed his bottom. When Berk turned around, Nina pointed at Georgina and said *'she did it'*.

That was that. The lover's eyes met over the kebab-on-a-platter. Georgina *really started living*. Except, this time, there were just too many people to lie to. Georgina lied to Kevin. She lied to her mother. She lied to the person answering the phone when she called in sick. Worst of all, she lied to those three innocent babies, who were now old enough to dress and feed themselves. She was spotted. Seen with a tan. Seen with a man. Seen getting into a taxi that looked like a van. As I said before, it is challenging to get sacked from a job in the NHS. However, it is relatively easy to get sacked by your Turkish waiter boyfriend. Her affair with Berk, (the man of strength) was over before it had properly begun. Maybe I have got the meaning wrong, Berk might really mean '*left too soon*' but that sort of naming would not, I imagine, be popular amongst males.

'Kevin will forgive me' Georgina said to herself while sucking a Turkish cigarette, 'He's a pussy'. But Georgina was wrong. In an absent-minded fashion, she opened her Facebook page. Scrolling through the usual stories of holidays, gin-drinking and pity parties, Georgina noticed a friend request- *who the hell is Shania Goatshed?* Georgina clicked on the woman's profile. She looked older and fatter than her (well everyone did to Georgina). And this woman was friends with all three of Georgina's children, and their father, Kevin. She accepted the friend request with meaningless interest. You can tell a lot about a person by how many Facebook friends they have, Georgina had over a thousand. Over the following week or so, Georgina tried to worm her way back into Kevin's devotions. But something was different. Kevin was no longer taking any of her nonsense. And all of a sudden, for the first time, Georgina was being bullied; cyberbullied.

As September, turned into October, (each morning fragranced with foreboding) Georgina realised that Shania Goatshed had not only trolled every one of her social media accounts but had also stolen her common-law husband!

When Kevin upped and left, Georgina had nowhere to live. She stayed with her mother, Pauline, who of course was not really dead, but really was Edith's ex-colleague. (See, I told you Edith would be upset). However, it was not long before Pauline decided she could not live with her horrid daughter. So, Georgina needed an alternative place to stay, enter Number One Curmudgeon Avenue!
I did warn you, reader, nincompoops and intertwined lives...

Samantha Henthorn

Chapter 25: The Dragon Enters The Tiger's Mouth.

Henri the Third's funeral came and went without a hiccup, and without Madame Genevieve Dubois. She never did return Edna's telephone call, and Edna was too proud to try again. (Not to anyone living, Edna did telephone in secret to no avail, this time using a secret code that would hide her number).

All the funeral guests had great fun and had plenty to say. Edna and Edith soberly watched them slowly drink themselves into oblivion... it was hilarious. Ricky Ricketts drunkenly interviewed his mother about being a *'Vulnerable Adult, just like Wantha's mum.'*

Anyway, I am meant to be telling you another tale now, a significant one. This is where the fun really starts.

A *meet-cute* they call it in the film world. When cupid's arrow strikes lucky, stars align, and fate shows its hand. This, however, is the story of when Harold met Edith. The red sky in the morning was not only a shepherd's warning, but the universe spoke to Edith, foretelling the rest of her unhappily married life. Edith being Edith, of course, did not listen.

Today, of all days, Edith decided to take up a new occupation-slash-hobby. She could no longer face the knitting circle after the Maurice incident. It was full of domestic goddesses. Their smug satisfaction of finished garments for their other-half was getting Edith down. She had always liked reading, although Edith had not picked up a novel for quite some time, most would say for longer than is reasonably necessary. The only recent reading list Edith could boast was a book that Ricky had vandalised and a pile of women's magazines, where salacious themes are forbidden. Today, Edith was going to return to the escapism, thrills and intrigue that only a *proper* novel can provide.

'Edna! Edna!' she called up the stairs to her sister, who of course ignored her, Edna was busy catching up on her correspondence via social media. (And watching the occasional funny cat video on YouTube). 'Which pair of tights are yours? I can never tell...' Edith was unravelling pantyhose from the clean laundry pile... Up and down the country, co-habiting women all have this problem (if they wear tights). Sisters, lovers, mothers and daughters, there is no way of telling which pair belongs to whom after they have been through the wash.

'Mine are the long ones, and yours are the short ones, surely Edith.' Edna shouted, reacting only to Edith for fear of her underwear being stolen by her sister.

'They don't make them in short and long... just small, medium or large!' It was futile entering into a discussion with Edna about tights, Edith had to make a stab of a guess. Pulling on the pair she was holding, fabric laddered up and down her corned beef calves - oh drat! Not to be put off her mission, Edith decided on a wardrobe change. Today would be pants... white pants. It was a shame that Edith had not thought the entire wardrobe through - and I am starting to see that the universe's warning was not really her fault. Edith strode out on that sunny morning wearing white trousers, (unflattering for her figure) with black knickers clearly visible through the cheap fabric. They had frayed at the backs of her hems due to vain denial of her small stature. This was about to be the least of Edith's worries when she presented her library card at Whitefield Library.

'Have you changed your address without telling us Mrs Ricketts?' the librarian asked in warm tones. (They are like that, librarians, friendly, even if you have forgotten to give them your new address). Edith clenched her brazenly rounded buttocks at the thought of being told off, she remembered she had not changed her address back to Curmudgeon Avenue. She opened her mouth to speak, but the librarian beat her to it.

'Only, we've got some overdue books here. Looks like you owe the library some money.'

'Huh!' Edith squeaked... this would not have happened if she had stayed at home with her cancelled subscription to the monthly 'tell me another one' women's magazine.

'Nothing to worry about, let's see if there's something we can do, this happens all the time. Don't worry.' The librarian could see that Edith was worried, but refused to allow the council to scare her off. That's the thing with librarians, if they meet someone wishing to share in the joy of reading, they go out of their way to nurture it. 'Now, I'll print off a form for the missing books, and then we can sort something out.'

'Books, plural?' said a worried Edith.

'Books, several' the librarian looked at the long list on her computer screen and hurriedly altered her expression to one of indifference. 'I tell you what, I don't want you to have a wasted trip, what kind of books are your favourites?'

'Well, I used to love a good romance.'

The librarian's eyes flickered towards the list of missing books, none of them romantic.

'Oh, like the classics or erotic romance?' she winked a friendly wink at Edith.

'I mean like Mills and Boon - that was the last book I read.'

'Well, we do stock Mills and Boon published novels. According to our records, you've read them all. Never mind, you seem as though you're in the mood for stretching your horizons, how about stick with the romance, but try a newer author? I like this one Laura Barnard she's called. And I tell you what Edith, you'll laugh your socks off.' Edith and the librarian soon became engrossed in a lengthy conversation about books...

By some strange coincidence, Harold was skulking around the library at the same time. To be honest, Harold was doing what most homeless and roofless people do, especially if it is raining, they hang around in libraries. He noticed Edith walk through the library doors, and it played on his mind. Harold recognised her from somewhere, but where? It occurred to him that he may have seen this woman when she was younger, much younger.

Harold sat on the comfortable chairs with today's newspaper positioned so that he appeared to be reading when actually, he was trying to listen to Edith's conversation. Then it dawned on him ... *It's the younger Payne sister*! One of the women he was trying to speak to the other day when Mrs Ali from the corner shop told him they were looking for a lodger! *Play it cool*, Harold thought to himself. *Should come naturally, of course to me*.

Harold's thoughts made him stand up from the

comfortable chair section of the library, and he edged... crept towards Edith and the librarian. The librarian, had never wanted to say the archaic term 'SHHHH!' more in all her career, because Harold was about to speak:

'I'm writing a book, you know...' he leaned on the library counter. If Edna had been here, she would be affronted, but Edith just giggled. Harold popped a stick of chewing gum in his mouth. He did not offer his gum to either woman. 'Yes. My life story, the things I've been through. I've had to leave some of the more recent stuff out of course...'

(Harold had a vague reminder of a driving job that went horribly wrong near Morecambe Bay a few years ago)

'Yes, my memoirs...' Harold looked off into the distance in a wistful, yet annoying way. The librarian had met Harold's type before. Get someone talking about books, and there is always some know-it-all in the room who announces they are writing one themselves. Harold was the worst kind of would-be author, the type that is writing a book about *himself.* The librarian knew how to deal with this situation.

'Oh, memoir writing is quite popular, you should have a word with the writing circle who meet here once a fortnight. Most people write memoirs for their family, not necessarily to be published. Unless you're famous, of course!' The librarian said, there was more giggling from Edith. Harold huffed a dismissive huff, he offered his last two sticks of chewing gum to Edith and the librarian. Just as Edith put out her hand to accept, the librarian stopped her. 'I'm sorry, I hope you don't mind me pointing this out, but we don't allow chewing gum in the library.'

Harold turned to leave, and Edith turned to follow him.

'What's your book called?' Edith asked in wide-eyed fascination.

'It's going to be called *The Dragon Enters the Tiger's Mouth*' Harold said, loudly enough for the librarian to hear...

'Sounds shit.' the librarian whispered under her breath and behind her counter.

Chapter 26: Goose Tape

Edith returned home with a long list of books allegedly borrowed but never returned to the library. That was the least of the troubles Curmudgeon Avenue was about to encounter; because Edith had Harold with her.

Harold set foot inside Number One Curmudgeon Avenue. He breathed in an unreasonable amount of air through his nose, Edith turned and looked up at him, if it were not for his nose hair, she would have been able to see his brain with the size of those nostrils.

'Edna! Edna! I've solved all our problems!' Edith was still looking at Harold, (quite adoringly, I must warn you). 'Edna! Can you hear me? I've found a lodger! ... It's Harold!'

That walk home had greased the cogs of both Harold and Edith's cerebral cortex. They do say that smells can often be a trigger for memories. When Harold put his arm around Edith to guide her away from a puddle, he treated her to a whiff of L'odour du Harold. That's when she had recognised him. By the time they had completed their short walk from Whitefield Library to Curmudgeon Avenue, Edith had practically given Harold her spare key. And Harold had almost wet himself with the stroke of fortune he had encountered today.

Meanwhile, Edna ignored Edith's shouting from downstairs. She was having a lovely time with Georgina Foote, the potential tenant and her mother, Pauline, (Edith's ex-colleague and enemy).

'This is the main bathroom' Edna gestured towards

the bright blue resin suite, it smelt of damp towels. Georgina was not impressed. 'And this will be your bedroom.' Edna opened the creaky door to Georgina's potential rental. You had to feel sorry for her. She had gone from suburban comfort to Turkish fantasia to a back bedroom in Curmudgeon Avenue. She tried not to breathe in. Her mother, Pauline, said that she needed to sit down. She walked with a stick, on no one's advice but her own, because Pauline was crumbling under her own weight.

'Did you just hear my hip when you opened that door?' Pauline said.

'That was the door creaking I think, not your hip, here, sit on this chair.' Edna said, immediately regretting the wicker chair suggestion. Pauline plonked herself down. Ever since Edith retired on the sick, Pauline has been trying to go down the same road herself. What a thing to be jealous of!

'No, it was definitely my hip, anyway Georgina, I think you should take it. It's very reasonable, and you'll be better off with women - not men! Stay away from men for a bit!' Pauline whispered the words *'she's got whore's blood coursing through her veins, this one'* for Edna to hear while she nodded at her daughter. The upstairs conversation continued in a similar fashion until Pauline had bullied her daughter into accepting the tenancy.

Meanwhile, Harold was downstairs with Edith, only half listening to what she was going on about, the other half of him was weighing up the situation. The house was bigger inside than he had imagined. He had only been through the door once before when he had taken Edna out on a date, many moons ago.

This is how Harold remembered what happened:

To be honest, Edna was not Harold's type. He was just grateful that she said yes. He only asked her out because he could, because no one else would (go out with Harold). Edna had insisted on meeting up during the day, and on this day the sky was sky blue. Harold suggested a ride out to the country. *'An adventure'* he persuaded her. Harold had forgotten his lie about owning a car - and may have told Edna he drove a mini. So when Harold turned up with a tandem, Edna turned her nose up. Harold remembered being slightly perturbed at Edna, *ungrateful cow,* he had stolen that tandem especially for her. Harold remembered taking Edna to a pub in the countryside, now what was it called? And how was Harold to know they would end up gate-crashing the wake of the chairman of the local bird-watching club? Harold had an arm wrestle with a man-on-crutches. Harold felt sorry for him and let him win. And the date ended with the pair passionately canoodling in the corner of the pub...

'Harold?' Edith said. She had been upstairs investigating Edna's whereabouts, while Harold was day-dreaming about Edna in the front room. Making himself at home on the leatherette settee. 'Come on, I'll show you around, Edna's upstairs somewhere. She says she has already found a lodger. It's all a bit awkward.'

'Already found a lodger?'
(How Harold stopped himself from admitting he had stolen Edna and Edith's advert out of Mrs Ali's window is beyond me).

'This is the under-the-stairs cupboard, Harold, it's where I go to chill out when Edna is getting on my nerves.' Edith did a little wiggle of her hips when she said *'chill out'*.

'Oh?' Harold said, quizzically raising one thick eyebrow.

'Oh, I mean it's where I go to chill out, so it's my private space really.' Edith immediately regretted giving too much away. Harold privately rubbed his hands together at the potential conflict. Poor Edith, she does not realise, if she does let Harold live at Curmudgeon Avenue she'll be spending a lot more time in that under-the-stairs cupboard. He's so annoying. Edith and Harold made their way through the house. At the same time, Edna, Pauline and Georgina continued their tour of Number One Curmudgeon Avenue. It may seem ridiculous that the two separate parties would not bump into one another. Still, with a bit of anti-clockwise shuffling in a four-storey Victorian terrace, Edna managed to avoid Harold.

'So am I OK to move in then? I've brought all my stuff with me' Harold sniffed. Edith looked down at the sad little ripped carrier bag - a bag for life that the supermarket refused to replace. 'The housing officer sent me, so you kind of have to let me move in.' he lied.

'Err, I'd just better check with Edna' Edith was rubbish at making decisions.

'Yes, you don't want to end up in the naughty cupboard.'

Now, that was very cheeky of Harold, but it made Edith giggle like a teenager.

'Oh, she doesn't put me in there... I put myself in there... to chill out!' Edith said, her flushed, fat face and sharp nose beamed up at Harold. He looked down at her big watery eyes. Harold thought Edith looked a bit like a comedy cartoon owl - a sweaty one.

'Where is Edna then?' Harold embarrassed Edith with his impatience, who was now worried that Harold was only interested in Edna. What a thing to be jealous of! I don't know what came over Edith, hopefully not the first flush of love, but from the other side of the serving hatch, Edith could be heard shouting:

'EDNA, IS A LESBIAN!'

The people that heard this were Pauline, Georgina Foote and Edna herself. Momentary wide-eyes were followed by Edna stepping forwards, swinging the serving hatch door open, smacking Harold in the face and knocking him to the floor. Thus proving his theory of sisterly tensions.

'Who's a lesbian? Hmm?' Edna berated her sister. Knowing this was rhetorical, Edith's hands itched towards the under-the-stairs cupboard. Harold was unconscious and oblivious.

'Harold wants to move in today.' Edith squealed and pointed at his lifeless body.

'Well so does Georgina Foote, don't you Georgina?' Edna shouted at Edith without looking at her potential tenant.

'Well I ...' Georgina started to say something, but her mother, Pauline hit her in the shin with her wooden walking stick.

'She can move in today.' Pauline said. Edna looked down at Georgina's sad little pink case on wheels. She had to borrow it from one of her children after the Berk the Turk episode. There ensued much arm folding and talking over each other, like any Tuesday morning at Curmudgeon Avenue. Still, this time, Georgina Foote was being shoved into the vacant bedroom by her (supposedly) disabled mother. And

Edith was being dragged up to the loft room by Edna. 'There's something I need to tell you about Harold' Edna whispered.

'Is it his funny smell? Do you think that's because he's been living in a homeless hostel? His sister robbed him of his inheritance, you know.' Edith said. Oh dear, she was already feeling sorry for Harold, already under his spell. Edna felt like slapping her across the face.

'No, Edith, it's from before, from you know - when we were young.' Edna was about to admit to Edith the story of Harold's brush with the law. Admit to her teenage lie in the phonebox on Stanley Road, but Edna was not sure where to start. Time was of the essence because they had a philanderer and her disabled mother in one room. And an unconscious homeless man on their kitchen floor. Edna flared her nostrils and opened her mouth to speak, but before any words could come out, a drop of rain that had seeped through the ceiling dropped right in it.

'Oh, see I told you that duct tape wouldn't hold!' the two sisters had spent the best part of Saturday morning taping up the dilapidated ceiling. The plaster had bulged every time it rained. Edith had insisted that 'Duct Tape' was called 'Goose Tape'. Nevertheless, Edith had a brainwave.

'Why don't we let them both move in? We'll get the money more quickly for the roofers. Doubly quickly.'
Edna thought about it. A flashback to that countryside pub; Harold had tried to snog her in the corner, and she had protected her face with her long hair. Edna shuddered, she would have to hide away in her bedroom trying never to bump into Harold. Even

Edith would get sick of him, Edna could almost guarantee it.

'Well?' Edith pleaded at her older sister, she knew that a compromise was the only way forward. Edna made a snap decision (she was good at them)...

'Ok then, we'll give it a try.'

Georgina Foote lay on the floor in the spare bedroom, underneath her mother who had wrestled her to the carpet, keeping her in a stranglehold. 'Where do I sign?' Pauline said on Georgina's behalf, and the tenancy was settled. Edna let Edith sort Harold out with a spare key, and so on. He would have to accept the 'other' spare bedroom, the one with all the rubbish in.

Just when the dust was about to settle on Curmudgeon Avenue, the front door knocker rattled again, and a set of brown teeth appeared at the frosted glass. It was Ricky Ricketts.

'Mum! Mum!' He shouted through the letterbox 'Wantha's thrown me out again - can I stay here for a few nights?'

Edith looked at Edna, and Edna pursed her lips.

Chapter 27: Is Nothing Sacred?

'Hellooo Edna? Edith? Hello, darlings, I made you a casserole...' Mrs Ali shouted through the letterbox of Number One Curmudgeon Avenue. She could not remember a time when the street was so busy. New lodgers, roofers, Ricky Ricketts staying until Wantha takes him back. 'Hello!' she rattled.

Inside, the hair inside Harold's nostrils began to twitch. He had always been very good at sniffing out free food. He had stolen food from his housemates up until now, waiting until Georgina had gone to work, or Edith had gone out. Ricky Ricketts, despite being skint, was constantly getting drunk and ordering takeaways. Harold had not seen much of Edna and enjoyed the fact that she was ignoring him.

Mrs Ali stood back in shock and delighted surprise when Harold swung the front door open and reached for her casserole dish. Mrs Ali quickly put her tea-towel back over the top. 'Oh, hello, darling.'

'Hello, Mrs Ali' Harold almost snatched the food out of her hands.

'So you did move in then?' Mrs Ali knew precisely who had moved in, she knew everything. 'This casserole is for Edna and Edith really, are they in?' Mrs Ali and Harold kind of circled one another, Harold reaching for the dish, and Mrs Ali putting her head inside the door frame.

'You can give it to me, I'll put it in the kitchen.' Harold said. He meant to put the entire contents of the casserole dish in his own stomach. It was only fair, he did not know where his next meal was coming from. This was not part of the deal as far as Mrs Ali was concerned. Her curried casserole was the currency for gossip, that's how it had always worked on Curmudgeon Avenue. In actual fact, up and down the country, the giving and receiving of leftover food often had an agenda and being a bachelor, Harold was wise to this.

'Wotcha, Mrs Ali, is your shop not open? I need some fags.' Ricky Ricketts squeezed past Harold while putting his arms in his greasy leather jacket.

'Oh, err I'll have to come back with you.' Mrs Ali said in a fluster. Somehow, Harold had managed to get hold of the casserole dish. Dismayed, Mrs Ali set off to return to her corner shop. As the front door closed, she heard a noise.

'Psst, psst, Mrs Ali!' from the upstairs front loft window, Edna whispered a secret message to her neighbour. 'I'll try and come round ... I can't stay in this room forever... the roofers will be here in a minute!'

'She's bonkers' Ricky Ricketts smirked 'I'm sure she's trying to hide from Harold.'
Mrs Ali could not wait for Edna to arrive so she could hear the full story.

'Do you sell flowers, Mrs Ali? I'm trying to cheer Wantha up.'

'So she will take you back again? No, I don't sell flowers, but I have after dinner mints on special, I bought in a job lot when that Maurice was visiting, but then he tried to murder your Auntie Edna. He doesn't come round anymore' Mrs Ali said, reaching for the mint chocolates. Ricky Ricketts did not bat an eyelid at the prospect of someone wanting to murder Edna.

'Why have you fallen out with Wantha this time?' Mrs Ali said, reaching for the cigarettes.

'Oh, she's stupid. I borrowed my mum's library card, and she didn't like the books that I was reading. I got that *50 Shades of Grey* - I thought I was romantic. She didn't like it. Then, the other books, well just because they were about men who either murdered their wives or have affairs, she thought I was doing research!'

'And were you?'

'No, I told you, she's an idiot, she threw those books in the paper recycling bin, she's an idiot!' Ricky Ricketts left the shop, in search of his idiotic on/off girlfriend... *Is nothing sacred*? Mrs Ali said to herself...

'Psst!' Edna summoned Mrs Ali to the back of her own shop where later that same day, the gossip commenced.

'Oh so he's Whitefield's unrelenting flasher?!' Said Mrs Ali, of course, she had heard plenty of whispers about it all those years ago. Today she was delighted to find that the man in question was Harold and that Edna had made the whole story up for revenge. 'He can eat fast too! Can't believe he polished off that entire chicken casserole all to himself!' Edna had been paid in emergency samosas in exchange for the full story.

'And I haven't even filled you in about Georgina Foote yet!' said Edna.

'No need, darling! My son knows someone from the Turkish restaurant, there's a cafe at the cash and carry, he hears all sorts of gossip there.'

'Well, she is a shadow of her former self if you ask me. The way her mother drop kicked her to the floor and kept her lying there ... she used to be a ward sister... I suppose Georgina can chew carpet like any other person can...'

'Now darling, be nice.' Mrs Ali said 'Did you know that your nephew Ricky Ricketts has stolen his mother's library card?'

'No I did not!' Edna protested 'But it doesn't surprise me he'll steal anything that isn't nailed down.'

'And he used the card to get pornography!'

'From the library?' Edna's voice was shrill, her nostrils quiver-some.

'Well, a mucky book, I won't stock it in my establishment...' Mrs Ali threw her silk shawl over her shoulder in disgust.

'I should think not Mrs Ali, I mean, is nothing sacred?'

'I know darling.'

'No wonder Edith was all upset and flustered when she came home from the library.'

'No. Edith was flustered because Harold is her new fancy man... I was minding my own business, swilling buckets out on the street.'

'Naturally,' agreed Edna.

'And I heard your sister giggling like a schoolgirl. Laughing at anything that man said! I could hear her before I saw her' Mrs Ali folded her arms. 'I'm telling you, Edna, cupid's arrow has struck on Curmudgeon Avenue and has tied your sister and *that man* together.'

'Oh' flopped Edna 'Nothing is sacred.'

Mrs Ali and Edna looked out onto the street, in the sunlight, they saw the silhouette of Harold stalking past the shop.

Chapter 28: Any Excuse to Get Wasted

On this day, the sky told a story of tipsy time-wasting.

'I've had to steal food from my flatmates. How would you like that? How would you like it if I had to steal food from you, young lady?' Harold picked Keeley Brimstone's egg salad muffin from her desk and shook it in her face.

'Mr Goatshed. Please take a number from the contraption on the wall, and wait your turn.'
Poor Keeley Brimstone. Harold should not really have been her problem now that he had a roof over his head, she was covering the duty desk when Harold turned up. One of her colleagues, Shirley (older and therefore slightly superior) had altered the rota in her own favour, but to Keeley's disadvantage. It seemed Keeley would never be rid of Harold, despite his recent tenancy agreement. Providing shadows of hope - hope that Harold would never darken Keeley's desk again. Yet here he was, once again on the other side of her diary and documents.

'I've got no money, Miss Brimstone, no Universal Credit.' Harold's neck wobbled like a turkey. He then said something that introduced the fear of another few months of him hanging around the housing department. 'I'm about to be kicked out of my new digs. They won't want me at Curmudgeon Avenue if I can't pay rent. Then I'll be homeless again, you'd like that wouldn't you, Miss Brimstone!'

'No, I most certainly would not, Mr Goatshed.' Keeley would not usually help the likes of Harold. But at the promise of being rid of him, she was prepared to telephone the mystery hotline that would ensure his benefits were reinstated on that very same day. Harold did not know how lucky he was about to be. 'Just wait here please, Mr Goatshed.'

After confirming that she had Harold's permission to speak on his behalf, the phone call was completed in private. The residents of Radcliffe queued behind Harold, and if Keeley revealed access to the mystery benefits hotline, she would never get off that duty rota. Keeley returned to her desk and could not contain her smile. She was about to speak to Harold for the very last time. So, during the time it took her from putting the telephone down to walking towards her desk, Keeley prepared a little speech.

'I have to confess, Mr Goatshed, the first time I saw you -'

'You were attracted to me, weren't you?' Harold interrupted, and Keeley was affronted, but her nerves made her burst out laughing.

'No. Mr Goatshed, I was not attracted to you that is not what I was going to say. Never mind, everything is in order, and I'm closing your case.'

'Everything's in order?'

'Yes, everything's in order, there is a cash point over the road.'

'Oh, I could kiss you!' Harold started to show his warmer side.

'No thank you, Mr Goatshed, please step away from my line.'

And Harold did just that, leaving the social and housing office in Radcliffe, and as he did, he thought he heard cheering and applause. He could not help himself and positioned a little curtsey as he left.

'What time is it, Harold?' Ricky Ricketts peeled himself off the leatherette settee, his drool and jacket, making a sticky union.

'Are you asking me?' Harold popped his head into the front room. Ricky Ricketts was still hanging around Curmudgeon Avenue like a smell in a bathroom.

'Yeah, there's no one else here, is there? That Georgina has gone to work, and Mum has gone to... oh somewhere.' speaking of smells, Ricky Ricketts was greeted by Harold sitting down with his legs at right angles. 'Where have you been?' Ricky breathed through his mouth.

'Oh, just to sort out my err, you know.'

'It's benefits day, isn't it?'

'Is it?' Harold hated people asking him about money.

'Yeah, everyone knows it. I'm meant to be meeting Wantha at the pub in half an hour, you coming?'

'Well, I'm meant to be paying my rent. What time is your mum coming back?'

'I can't remember what she said, by the time she had gone round the houses with what she was telling me. Anyway, that's not a thing, you can't refuse to come to the pub because you're paying your rent. Just leave it in the Butlin's tin, that's what that Georgina one does.'

'Well, I suppose I could write my name on an en-vlope.'

'A what?'

'An en-vlope'

'You say it funny, Harold. You could go and find Aunty Edna. I've not seen her going out.' Ricky looked as though he was really concentrating on the whereabouts of Edna. Harold shuddered at the sound of her name.

'What is it with you two anyway?' Ricky Ricketts was quite observant considering his useless status.

'What is it with us two?' Harold started his sentence dramatically, but thought better of it and changed the subject 'We'd better go to the pub if we need to get there for half-past.'

After she heard the front door close, Edna crept out of her bedroom and counted Harold's rent. She then washed her hands in very hot water, because she had touched something that Harold had touched. Harold and Ricky Ricketts walked to the Frigate pub in Whitefield, where there was any excuse to get wasted. Such as today, being a Tuesday - what better excuse than to get blind drunk? And how romantic too! Harold and Ricky Ricketts formed a 'bromance' over a few (twelve) pints. Someone had to be on their respective sides.

'I thought you said... what was her name? Your lady friend is meeting us here?' Harold said to Ricky, he had not yet settled into his drunken comfort and twitched every time someone walked through the door.

'Lady-friend!' Ricky Ricketts laughed 'I love you, Harold, you say things funny. You mean Wantha?' Ricky Ricketts punctuated his man-chat with sups of lager. 'This is what she does, she is making me pay. It's all mind games with her. She is threatening me with the *Jeremy Kyle Show*, wants a lie detector and a DNA test and the audience booing at me.'

'A DNA test? What for?'

'She wants it all, and I give it all, but then she falls out with me over something daft. I was only trying to spice things up, Harold, I'm just a man, but she kicked off when she saw that I had got that book *50 Shades of Grey* out.' Ricky Ricketts sighed a deep sigh. Harold twitched an uncomfortable twitch.

'Well, in my experience, women prefer the gentler approach. Why don't you try 'Seven Shades of Grey' instead, you know, to start off with...' Harold said, (and pah! I know what you are thinking. As if Harold knows anything about women!)

'Seven Shades of Grey? That's not a thing Harold' The more Ricky Ricketts laughed, the more brown teeth he showed 'No, she does this, she arranges to meet, makes me wait and then I'm back in there. Mum's settee will be history this time tomorrow- trust me.'
Harold *was* starting to trust Ricky Ricketts, which was the trouble with the Frigate pub.

'Anyway, what do you mean? In your experience? I thought you'd never been married - unless...' Ricky Ricketts threw back his head in mocking laughter, showing all of his fillings, barely visible amongst his darkened teeth 'You forgot to finish telling me about you and Auntie Edna.'

Just then, the door of the pub flung open revealing the image of the two mismatched sisters, Wantha and Toonan. Wantha was wearing a bright yellow fake fur bomber jacket which matched her hair and silver jeggings. Toonan wore her trademark shell-suit.

'Alright' Wantha said.

'Wantha, you're late' Ricky Ricketts winked a seedy wink at Harold.

'No!' Wantha lifted her forefinger upwards towards Ricky Ricketts' face. 'Do not give me any chit-chat.'

'Who's your friend?' Toonan thumbed towards

Harold.

'This is Harold. He's my mum's lodger, and he was about to tell me about how he used to go out with my Auntie Edna.'

'OMG! This, I have to hear! Get the drinks in Ricky!' Toonan made herself comfortable.

'Hang on is that the house that we tried to move into? And they let *YOU* move in instead of *US?*' Wantha made that clicking noise with her tongue and the roof of her mouth. 'Get the shots in, *HAROLD!*' Wantha sat down next to Ricky Ricketts and batted Harold off in the direction of the bar. Just then, Patchouli, (Wantha and Toonan's mother) walked in. Now, Patchouli had never spoken to Harold before, but she had lived in Whitefield all her life. And so knew all the gossip over the years.

'Hiya Harold love, I never believed all that gossip about you being a sex pest' Patchouli said, before joining her wide-eyed chuckling daughters.

Chapter 29: Ruminations of Revenge.

Mrs Ali was usually right about her predictions. It had been a huge shock and disappointment to her when Mr and Mrs Payne (Edna and Edith's parents) were crushed to death by an elephant. Mrs Ali had spent the previous six months telling them not to visit the zoo, and to get the brakes tested on their car. Sadly, Mrs Ali's predictions were slightly wrong. But what if she was right this time? What if Edith was to get together with Harold? Edna would have to move, she could not hide in the loft conversion forever.

One thing that Edna and Edith had not reckoned on was that they would have to share a bedroom while the roof was being fixed. There was plenty of extra foot traffic and bedroom space required at Number One Curmudgeon Avenue for Harold, Ricky Ricketts and Georgina Foote.

On this particular night, when the sky was as purple as one of those famous chocolate wrappers, both Edna and Edith were having trouble sleeping. Edith could not sleep because of Edna's snoring, loud apnoea barking snores. And when Edna was not snoring, she was farting loud and guttural farts (yes, farts that sounded as though they had started in her throat). Edna herself was having what some people call a fitful night's sleep. She was dreaming of Harold, or rather she was 'nightmaring' about Harold (although I do not think that is a word). Ruminations of the past can often play havoc with a person's equilibrium in the early hours. The two sisters lay side by side, not sleeping but not speaking either. Edith wishing for silence, Edna, thinking about the past. Her worries went *way* back.

It all started when their parents became uppity about which high school Edna would attend. Mr and Mrs Payne refused to allow their eldest daughter to attend the secondary modern and Edna Payne became a grammar school girl. However, when it was little Edith's turn for high school, Mr and Mrs Payne, (disappointed with Edna's progress) sent Edith to the school that everyone else went to. This gifted Edna a life lesson, for no one's benefit but her own. Edna's grammar school days taught her nothing more than that she was better than her sister, better than everyone else, better without even trying. She left school with no qualifications, and only the art teacher liked her.

All though going out of fashion, marriage had been an option for the unskilled woman, and the next male specimen that Edna saw was none other than Harold Goatshed. And now Edna, unable to sleep remembered one of their disastrous dates...

'Hubba hubba, Edna' Harold leaned against the kitchen door while biting into a stolen apple. Edna had made sure she squashed her bosom towards Harold when putting her shoes on. This was long before the days of turtle necks and long before Edna had left home.

'Edna, peel those apples before you go out won't you' Mother said. 'There's just enough for eve's pudding.' But then she stopped in her tracks 'Hang on! I'm one short!' All eyes turned on Harold and his half-eaten apple. 'That's a cooking apple. My cooking apple! It's meant to be cooked! I hope it gives you wind!

Harold blushed, and Edna smirked, they left Curmudgeon Avenue, leaving Mrs Payne to peel her own apples. Then Edith revealed that she had been in the under-the-stairs cupboard all the time.

'Where are we going?' Edna said as Harold led her off the road down a cobbled path.

'Harold?'…'Hello?'…' Yoo-hoo'

Harold could hear Edna but decided to ignore her. It was pointless to have a conversation until they had stopped walking. Poor Edna was out of breath. Her black eye makeup streaked down her face. 'We're going to meet up with someone in here' Harold thumbed towards the Golden Gate pub. When males say 'someone', not always, but usually, this means an ex-girlfriend. Another lesson for Edna. Still, for the time being, she had to look at Harold's shiny scalp under his bristling black hair as they entered the dimly lit drinking establishment.

'Hello Sweetheart!' a woman with bottle-blonde hair and fake confidence addressed Harold.

'He-hey! He-hello Barbara' Harold sort of laughed as he spoke, in a pompous and cheesy fashion. Harold and Barbara looked into each other's eyes for quite some time. Harold, with lust, Barbara with the fondness of the 'friend-zone'. Edna stood there as awkward as a bunion.

'Let me get the drinks in' Harold fished out his moth-eaten wallet from his back pocket.

'Wait!' Barbara screeched, holding her right hand vertically in Edna's direction. 'Who... is this?' she gushed towards Edna, almost knocking her over.

'Ah' Harold's head wobbled. 'This, is Edna. And do you know, Barbara, when I first saw her, I said to

myself 'Hubba-Hubba' Harold, she won't be
interested in *me*'...
(Now, at the time, Edna thought this was sweet, but
when remembering this particular date with Harold,
Edna was fuming. Harold had only gone out with
Edna to make Barbara jealous. And it did not have the
desired effect).

'Oh, you are cute, Harold' Barbara said, placing
her hand gently on his forearm. 'I've known him
since high school. Look at you two, so cute together.'

'Anyway, about those drinks, ' Harold said.

'Oh, you must have a Babycham darling.
Everyone's drinking it' Barbara told Edna what to
have.

'I doubt they'll serve Babycham in here' Edna
said, observing the distinct working men's vibe.

'Well, why don't you ask them?' Harold said,
smacking his lips together like a rubber band.

'Run along then' Barbara shooed Edna away to the
bar.

Edna did ask, and no, they did not serve
Babycham, even though it was the 1980s. Had Harold
just tricked Edna into buying the drinks? Typical
bloody Harold. When she returned from the bar,
Harold and Babycham Barbara were deep in
conversation. Harold sat with his legs at a right angle,
his elbow rested on the table. His knuckles held up
his face, forming a triangle that kept Edna out of their
conversation. Harold was going on about stuff and
nonsense, proving his inflated view on conspiracy
theories by repeated assertion. Babycham Barbara
appeared to be placating him, and Edna could not get
a word in. She sat on one of those little bar stools,
unable to drag herself into the party without making

an awful scraping sound on the slate floor. Edna remained there, more like her little sister Edith, on the edge of the conversation. And let me tell you, this was the last time that Edna Payne allowed this to happen. Ever. From then on, Edna would not speak to anyone unless she got the chance to talk about how talented and beautiful she was, but not on this night...

Edna was now wide awake and fuming in her revenge ruminations *'Bloody Harold!'* she shouted out in frustration.

'Are you OK, Edna?' Edith said from her side of the bedroom.

'Yes, oh, I was having a nightmare' Edna lied and ran her tongue over her teeth, tasting her own morning breath. They both heard a tapping at their bedroom door.

'Hello,' the tapping sound said 'Is everything OK in there?'

'Yes, thank you!' Edna said in uppity tones.

'Only I heard someone shouting my name!' Well, that was just typical of Harold. Edna rolled her eyes, and Edith blushed.

Chapter 30: You'll Never Sell Curmudgeon Avenue, Not in a Million Years.

You may be forgiven for thinking that all was rosy at Number One Curmudgeon Avenue. The roof was getting fixed, Edith was warming to Harold in the same way that Edna had warmed to him all those years ago. Georgina Foote was a paying, and reliable tenant and Ricky Ricketts' relationship continued to bumble along in the dramatic way that the young folk of Whitefield enjoy so much these days. But do not let yourself think that Edna is happy! She would be nothing without that scowl.

Put yourself in Edna's shoes though; long term partner mysteriously disappears believed to be living in France - possibly with a Lancashire accent. Ex adopted son of long term partner tries to sue for his dubious adoption and lack of birth certificate, (the legal fees of which are left to Edna). Then her parents get squashed by elephants. Edna is forced to live with her irritating younger sister who falls in love with one of her childhood boyfriends - the most annoying Harold that ever lived! Not to mention the leaking roof. Poor Edna, this chain of events, would be enough to send anyone potty. Not Edna though, not to the outside world, and when I say outside, I mean outside her bedroom. As soon as the roofers had finished, she locked herself away, it was her way of dealing with the Harold situation.

Meanwhile, Edith remembered before she married Reginald Ricketts all those years ago. Someone told her that marriage meant she would spend her life picking up socks and underpants. Now, who was that? It was Edna. But what was Edith going to do about

Edna? Her older sister she lived with, feared the wrath of, but could not say when she had seen her last.

Edith asked Harold about Edna. What a mistake. This did nothing but massage his ego. Men like Harold could only dream of two sisters fighting over him. Even if he was stretching the truth.

'Why, what has Edna said?' Harold was looking at himself in the mirror, Edith sat behind him on her bed.

'Nothing! I haven't even spoken to her about you. Well apart from ages ago, you know, years ago' Edith dug herself further in, 'I think she might be hiding from us.'

'Oh,' Harold said. Edith could not tell if that was a grumpy 'oh' or a regular 'oh'. Maybe Harold is just cranky in the mornings.

Familiarity was breeding contempt. Harold and Edith were spending more and more time together. Edna was now fully isolated, she could go for weeks, and the only person she had seen was Mrs Ali - and that was out of the window. What else could Edna do? She was guilty of perverting the course of justice. Harold had been falsely accused of trespass... And even though no charges were brought - the mystery accuser (Edna) had failed to make further contact with the police, people thought of him as a pest, a nuisance ... It was only a matter of time before he traced it back to Edna. The longer she kept this a secret, the worse it got. She had talked herself out of any involvement, then talked herself back in again. She deserved it. That's what you get for holding a grudge for so many years. Now he was dating her poor little sister! Edna thought long and hard about this. She got herself all vexed. She could see how it was going to go. Harold was already *'throwing his weight around'* pinching food and changing the TV channel.

Edith, meanwhile could not cope without her older sister. *And* there was the guilt. Edith was falling in love with Harold, but this seemed to have sent Edna into a deep depression, hardly venturing out of her room. All because of Edith (or so she thought). She had read somewhere that not going out can cause a lack of vitamin D, and this could cause all kinds of problems. The other thing getting to Edith was that if Edna did not go out, Edith would have to do everything. All the cleaning and all the shopping. And deal with the up and over garage door alone.

Edith, concerned that Edna was having a breakdown wanted to help her before it was too late.

Edna, concerned that Edith's meddling would result in her secret being exposed. Needed to hide even further before it was too late.

Harold suggested writing a poem. 'She likes poems, I once wrote her a poem to help her understand why we had to break up.'
Edith thought of Harold's poem, how she had rescued it from the bin after Edna scrunched it up into a ball and threw it in there. Edith gave in, and wrote Edna a poem. The intention was, for Edna to realise she needed help.

Obsessive Compulsive Disorder
She made a fortress where she felt safe
Hoarding stuff right up to her face
Vermin got a warm embrace
What a mess
The neighbours complain
They don't know her shame
The isolation of self-inflicted pain
Obsessively counting over again
I've looked into this graded exposure
She doesn't want to recover, it's all she has control over.

Edith had added a bit of drama to the poem. No mice had been found in Edna's bedroom. Well apart from the dead one that Henri the third had put in the eaves (latterly discovered by the roofers). No neighbours had complained. Mrs Ali had mentioned something to Edith, but only out of concern. Yes, Edith added a bit of drama to the poem, but at least she made it rhyme. Edith, being Edith, gave the poem to Edna as an early birthday present. She slotted it inside a book of poetry. Edna failed to notice the piece of paper drop out of the book. She smiled at her sister.

'I've meant to speak with you, Edith' Edna came over all motherly and patronising. 'I've been worried about you... Look, if you are going to take up with Harold, just be careful he doesn't take advantage of you' Edna stood on the step that led into the attic room. And Edith was standing a few steps down from her.

'Take advantage?' Edith said, all thoughts of poems and graded exposure now out of the window 'I'm nearly seventy!'

'Oh, I didn't mean *that*, Edith. I meant money, that sort of thing. Harold, he has his ways. Always wants something for nothing, you know.'

'Well, he might be different with me.' Edith started to retreat down the stairs. Edna had manipulated Edith and touched a nerve.

'I think we should sell the house, Edith. Cut our losses and split the proceeds. Then you can do what you want with your share' by this, Edna meant Harold and Ricky Ricketts.

'You'll never sell this house, not in a million years!' said Harold from his eaves-dropping perch. Edna eventually asked for help, with her compulsions, but only because she thought this would provide a good defence if, indeed she was ever arrested for setting Harold up. Nothing came of it though. Edna was offered an appointment at the nearest mental health centre.

The letter read as follows:

Dear Miss Payne,
Your GP has referred you to the community mental health team to cure your fear of leaving the house.
Therefore, please leave your house, and attend the appointment on the date and time stated on the enclosed appointment card.
Yours sincerely
Georgina Foote RMN

There was no such appointment card enclosed. Edith telephoned to confirm the appointment time for her sister. She was told that Georgina Foote was; *'On the sick, long term due to stress'*... Georgina Foote? She's our lodger! Edna thought, had anyone seen her recently, though? All this concern for Edna's well-being and no one had noticed that Georgina Foote was missing!

Chapter 31: The Collective Noun for Fugitives.

'Psssst! Oi!' Edna summoned Mrs Ali when she popped out of her shop to swill her mop bucket on the pavement.

'Oh, hello, darling! Why don't you come round for a chai latte?'

'Shhh! Don't let Harold know you're talking to me!' Edna pulled her turtle neck up around her facial hair. Mrs Ali looked around her confusedly, there was no sign of Harold. 'Have you seen Georgina Foote recently?' Edna sort of shouted and whispered at the same time. Mrs Ali looked around herself again. 'You know, our lodger, blonde, big-boned?' Mrs Ali shook her head 'had an affair!' The penny dropped with Mrs Ali 'Ohhh I know who you mean. No! I haven't seen her for days, darling'...

Somewhere, on the stretches of railway tracks in Britain, two strangers, seated on uncomfortable corded train seats had more in common than they knew. '*You are a strong, confident woman'* Georgina repeated to herself, assuming these were her private thoughts. The older woman in the pink transparent Mac opposite her looked up with a start.

'Pardon Mademoiselle'

'Oh, I'm sorry, I don't speak French.'

'Sorry, I thought you said something.' her English speaking voice was noticeably more Lancastrian than Georgina Foote expected. She ran her fingers through her hair, and at the back of her head got one end of her flexible brass bangle caught. 'Are you going all the way to Scotland?'

'Oui' The French woman replied. Georgina rearranged her scarf and looked at the book she had brought, a book about feminism. Despite being a strong, confident woman, she felt too self-conscious to read this on the train. So instead, Georgina spent all the way from Manchester to Morpeth telling her life story, all about her grown-up children. That she was going to visit 'Trace', who had moved to Northumberland, one last time before leaving the country. 'Trace' does not like Georgina's lover, Berk, but what could Georgina Foote do? (Berk was back on the scene from Turkey and back in Georgina's affections).

'The heart wants what the heart wants' she said to the French woman digging long red fingernails gently into the other woman's forearm.

It was a long journey, and Georgina's train companion was feeling pressed to share a little of herself. Fortunately, Georgina was now going on about her obsession with spiritualists. She had spent a lot of money visiting mediums, searching for answers about if she should stay with Berk. Was he ever going to commit? And whatever would happen over Trace, and her reluctance to move back to Whitefield? Then Georgina Foote started talking about her last address in Whitefield. (Omitting the bit about stealing the rent money.) And said something that made the other woman want to get off the train immediately and travel the opposite direction to Manchester.

'NEXT STOP NEWCASTLE. DOORS TO YOUR LEFT'

'That's me, nice to have met you' The French woman hurriedly collected her belongings together to flee the scene. She was getting quite used to running away; but when she heard Georgina say the words 'Curmudgeon Avenue', she made a snap decision to run home (well one of her homes).

Georgina waved at her nameless French companion through the train window as if she had known her for years. When the train pulled away from the station, Georgina noticed that the woman had dropped something on the floor. It was too late, the train now weaved its way further and further away from the train station. Georgina picked the lost property up anyway.

'A French newspaper? That woman sounded as though she had lived here for years! '*Le Figaro*' Oh, fancy that! Hang on a minute! That's her!' Georgina Foote was talking to herself and looking at a picture of her train companion.

'VEUVE NOIRE!'

Now even though it was a French newspaper, Georgina Foote could remember a little of her Castlebrook High School French. 'Oh, my God! Genevieve Dubious stands accused of being the black widow of Rocamadour! She's a fugitive! Just like me! Oh, and she was acting as though we had nothing in common! ... I wonder what the collective word for fugitives is?

Chapter 32: Ricky Ricketts, of all People, Phones the Police.

'I told you, didn't I?' Ricky Ricketts, when excited spat when he spoke.

'What? Told me what son?' Edith held the empty Butlin's fudge tin, the one she had been collecting the rent in.

'Not you, I told Auntie Edna.'
Harold, Edith and Ricky looked up towards the ceiling to indicate Edna's stalemate with her bedroom.

'People are going about taking advantage of women your age. I offered to get a protection order for both of you, but she wouldn't have it!' Ricky Ricketts spat.

'Hang on, did you see Georgina leave? I think you're jumping to conclusions' Harold's head wobbled.

'I said nothing, old man, where were you anyway? Hmm, my mum gets robbed blind, and you did nothing about it.'
Harold was folding his newspaper into angry little creases.

'Look, I've already been in her room, she's taken all her stuff and done one, with this month's rent money from her and Harold.'

'You shouldn't have been in her room! That's private!' Edith said 'And anyway, there's a lock on that door!'

'I know, I forced it open, it's not her room now, she's gone.'
Meanwhile, upstairs in her hidey-hole, Edna could hear the sound of raised voices and power struggles. She stuck her nose in the air and continued painting.

'Well, it could have been her room, what if all her stuff was still there and she came back and denied stealing the rent?' Harold said.

'Well, then we'd be looking at you Ha-rold!' Ricky Ricketts said. 'Right, none of this standing around, I'm phoning the police!' Ricky Ricketts said (but not before placing his stash of cannabis resin in Harold's rucksack without his knowledge). On this particular day, when the sky looked like a pumice stone, there was only one police constable on duty in Whitefield. They don't give out their names, just collar numbers. So when constable Legend pedalled his push-bike down Curmudgeon Avenue, he was not expecting the likes of Ricky Ricketts greeting him at the door.

'What's your name, pal?' Ricky was chewing gum and generally being irritating.

'Errm... you rang the police? About a theft?' Constable Legend said. With a surname like that, the police force had seemed the perfect job for him.

'Yes we did, money, rent money has gone missing and - coincidentally, our lodger, Georgina Foote has gone missing at the same time!' Edna said, having slipped down the stairs when she heard the police arrive. She had mysteriously forgotten all about hiding from Harold at the temptation of getting to speak to an official. An official police officer that is. And mysteriously, Harold had disappeared on the same notion.

'Well, I'd better take some particulars down.'

'Listen, pal, it wasn't any of us' Ricky Ricketts looked around the room. He instinctively avoided mentioning the missing Harold, he knew when not to grass. 'It was that Georgina, no question, and she's done one, so on your bike, pal and get after her!'

'Would you like a cup of tea?' Edith piped up.

'Err, no thank you, I need to take some details, how many people are living in this house? I'll need to interview you all.'

Edith could not stop talking. There was no way the police officer needed to know how well she was doing on her diet, but she told him anyway.

'There's four of us' Ricky Ricketts said.

'Four?' asked Edith.

'Yes, well, my official home is with Wantha.'

'Wantha?' Said the policeman.

'Yes, Wantha, her mum made it up.'

'What about Har' Edith started to say 'Harold.'

'HAVE you seen Georgina's room? I'll show you, there might be some clues' Ricky Ricketts guided the police officer upstairs. Away from his over-talkative mother and away from Harold. He had been right, Harold was hiding from the police. Locked away in his room, hoping that his face, his goggle eyes were not on some wanted poster in a police station somewhere. Wanted in connection with that traffic offence. Harold had been wanted by the police in his younger days (remember - it was Edna's fault) he knew how these people worked. And so did Ricky Ricketts, who kept this information in his pocket for a later date - right where he wanted him. Hidden Harold on the first floor was not the only fugitive that Curmudgeon Avenue was about to harbour.

'And this is my bedroom, officer, we had the luxury roof re-done recently' Edna always spoke as though she is better than everyone (which she is not).

'He's not coming on a viewing! He's coming over your stolen money Auntie Edna!'

'What's that noise?' said the policeman. They all

stopped silent, and there, the noise started again.

'It sounds like someone throwing pebbles at a window!' said Edith dramatically.

'Don't be ridiculous, Edith, it's probably something to do with our new luxury roof.'

'What? Making a noise?' patronised Ricky Ricketts. Fortunately, for the pebble thrower - Edna was nearest the window. She looked out, her eyes widened, her heart started thumping with love and countless other emotions. In that split second, she recognised Madame Genevieve Dubois, who, on arriving at her destination, had seen the police car and feared the worst.

'Shhh!' she signalled to her absent life partner, Edna. 'Don't let them see me!'

'Right well, you've seen the attic room, time to search the rest of the house' Edna used her full force to shoo her unwanted guests away.

Chapter 33: Radcliffe Hors d'oeuvres.

On the morning of this interlude, the sky just outside Edna's luxury skylight was filled with the sound of those annoying wood pigeons. You know, the ones that will not go away. Madame Genevieve Dubois ran her scarlet painted talons up and down Edna's tree-trunk legs. She grimaced at the flaky skin under her fingernails. Edna did not notice, she was wrapped up in the delight that her long lost lover had delivered to Curmudgeon Avenue.

Yesterday, Officer Legend gave the impression that the stolen rent money was lost forever, and the case would be closed. Regarding the 'Black Widow of Rocamadour,' intelligence from France failed to reach the 'MOST WANTED' board in Whitefield Police Station. Genevieve was quite safe under the luxury roof of Number One, Curmudgeon Avenue.

'I know you say you have been, but the two of us? Up here? Unnoticed?' Genevieve pouted about Edna's self-isolation.

'Ever since that imbecile who calls herself my sister moved *Harold* in, I've had no other option.' Edna said, in whispered tones. Ah yes, it was all coming back to Genevieve now, she heard *all* about Harold on the day of her first romantic exchange with Edna. As they lay there, the memories flooded in... Edna debated if she should tell Genevieve about Maurice, he was around in those days - and had even tried to murder Edna six months ago. (Which was a coincidence, because Genevieve was wanted for murder herself).

There had been nothing more sophisticated to Edna in the 1980s than having a French neighbour. She remembered the day they met like it was yesterday. The sky greyed by clouds that looked like a blackberry fool. And now Genevieve was back, returned to Curmudgeon Avenue... But Edna had no idea of her fugitive status.

'Maybe you're right, Genevieve. I'm sorry I said no last night, but it was just so sudden. Seeing you there on the street. I should have said yes...'

'You mean.... you're willing to leave Curmudgeon Avenue and be together again?' Genevieve purred. 'In France?'

'Well, it might not be the best day to make the...'

'Qu'est-ce que c'est?' Genevieve interrupted... (Edna could not resist that French accent).

'It's Edith's birthday today.' Edna explained. Poor Edna. That turtle neck jumper could not protect her now.

Meanwhile downstairs, Harold had a surprise for Edith. 'What time did you say everyone was coming round, Edith?'

'Oh I just got a text from Ricky, they're going to the off licence they shouldn't be long.'

'Well, I've got a surprise for you, Edith' Harold said, with a wobbly head.
Now in that snapshot... that moment... Harold wanted to know what time people were coming, why did he want to be alone with Edith? What's the surprise? Edith's mind naturally and incorrectly turned to marriage. Poor Edith, so many presumptions, all of them wrong.

'Edith, you've drifted off... how old did you say

you were this time?' Harold was as subtle as a brick.
'Are you ready for your surprise?'

'Yes, Harold.'

Harold disappeared into the kitchen, then bobbed his
head out with a 'pleased with himself' look on his
face. He reappeared in the front room brandishing a
dinner plate, as round as Edith's disappointed face.

'Are they *Mini Cheddars*?'

'Not just any old *Mini Cheddars*...' said Harold.

'And is that *Primula* cheese spread on top of
them?'

'These, Edith, are Radcliffe Hors d'oeuvres.'
Harold was so pleased with himself, he even
developed a French accent. (They had no idea that
this made two French accents in Curmudgeon Avenue
- how farcical!)

'Radcliffe what-you-say?' Edith said. All she could
see was crackers and cheese spread.

'Hors d'oeuvres! Try one Edith!'

And so Edith popped one of the cheap buffet fancies
in her tiny cakehole. It was surprisingly more-ish. She
took another, and Harold did something he should not
have. He smacked her hand.

'Don't be eating all the party food before everyone
has got here, Edith! I want everyone to see my
signature dish.'

Edith burst into tears. Where was Edna when she
needed her? She could just imagine her sister berating
Harold: '*Signature dish my arse!!*' But where was
Edna? Edith knew she had hidden from Harold. Even
so, Edna had managed a running commentary on
every self-righteous thing that Harold had done since
moving in. Right there, on Edith's birthday, it struck
her. Was she willing to suffer a life with Harold

smacking her hand without her sister Edna to protect her? And again, where was Edna? Harold meanwhile was waffling on with himself, offering Edith a stick of celery. Edith did not hear him. It was not until the guests let themselves in through the back door of Number One Curmudgeon Avenue (how uncouth!) That Edith re-joined the conversation.

'Alrite Edith!' said Toonan, greeting her as though she was a long lost auntie. 'They didn't have no Prosecco in the offy, so I had to get you Lambrini.' she announced her unwrapped gift to Edith, flopped down on the chair and cracked open a can of cider. (It was 11am). Ricky Ricketts entered the scene without even saying hello or happy birthday to his mother. His head was in the fridge.

'Did you not get the beers in, Harold?'

'That's your department, Ricky. You said you were going to the off-licence, I'm in charge of the buffet. Would you like a Radcliffe Hors d'oeuvres?'

'No thanks, Harold. I'm allergic to *Primula*. Remember, mum? Leroy Legre had to lend me a cheese and beetroot butty on the school trip to Chester Zoo. I came out in a rash near the penguins. It was all because his mum used *Primula*. Lazy cow, not grating proper cheese.' Ricky Ricketts turned his nose up at Harold's buffet, and all things processed. Edith nodded vaguely, her mind still on her missing sister.

'What's this about cheese butties? I'm starving' said Wantha, holding up the rear with her mother, Patchouli.'

'Radcliffe Hors d'oeuvres?' said Harold.

'Those are Whitefield Vol-au-vents. Actually, Harold' said Patchouli 'We used to put them together quick on Hillock when we had nothin' else in!'

Well, Edith's birthday party got into full swing.
Harold sent Edith out to the off licence for more
booze, and when she returned with her blue plastic
bag weighed down with wine, all the Radcliffe Hors
d'oeuvres had vanished. Mrs Ali arrived with
samosas, so all was not lost. It wasn't until they set
up a game of beer pong in the back yard, that Edna
appeared in a cloud of chiffon and silk scarves. Her
nose was exceptionally vertical today because of the
sorry scene unfolding at Curmudgeon Avenue.

'Here's your birthday present, Edith.'

'Oh, thanks, Edna! Where have you been hiding?'
Edith was so pleased to see her sister and gazed up
her nostrils with her very slightly boss-eyed stare.
Edith ripped open the rectangular-shaped parcel to
reveal a photo frame. Behind the glass, sat a face that
had been subject to one of those cheap makeovers and
was cuddled by a soft misty filter. The face was
perched on interlaced fingers holding up its chin. Far
too much makeup had been applied, particularly to
the slightly parted lips. There was no mistaking.
However, the upturned, nose right in the middle.
Edna had presented Edith with a framed photograph
of herself for her birthday...

'Something to remember me by Edith...' Edna said
in theatrical tones.

'Remember you? Are you dying Edna?' Edith
clutched the framed photograph of Edna, her sister
had finally joined her birthday party, and now she
was about to ruin it.

'No, Edith... I am moving to France!'

Acknowledgements and stuff...

Thank you to you, reader for putting up with Curmudgeon Avenue's whinging potty mouth, I apologise for the swearing. I am an independent author, this basically means it has been just you, me and Curmudgeon Avenue involved in this reading experience. With no big company behind me, I am without deadlines. But, I am also without fancy-pants editors and marketing budgets. It has been a really special moment that you have chosen to read Curmudgeon Avenue. If you enjoyed this book, why not share the love and let another reader know, either by word-of-mouth or leaving a review on Amazon or Goodreads.

Thank you to my actual real-life friends from Whitefield, Radcliffe and the surrounding areas. Some of them do frequent the local pubs from time to time. All events in this book are fictional – you are quite safe should you choose to visit. You will not bump into Harold, Ricky Ricketts or any of the other nincompoops.

Thank you to author Laura Barnard for allowing me to name drop her. What the fictional librarian said is correct, you will laugh your socks off if you read any of her books.

Thank you to Deborah J Miles of Against the Flow Press.

Thank you to my dashingly handsome husband, Mark, who embarrasses easily and rescued my laptop when I thought I had lost 'Curmudgeon Avenue'. At this point, I must also thank Radcliffe Pete too because he found the files that Mark couldn't...

Thank you to my daughter Alicia my dog, Martha and my two cats for disturbing me regularly during the writing process, you keep me real.

Thank you to my parents, Sylvia and Peter, for the constant supply of love and encouragement. Thank you to my brother, who gave me the idea for the names 'Toonan and Wantha'. It was how he used to pronounce mine and my sister's names when he was little.

Thank you to the real Whitefield writing circle, where Harold and Edith were 'born' in the first short story I ever wrote in 2014.

Curmudgeon Avenue has gone through several revisions, none so exciting as its transformation to audio by the multi-talented voice-over actor Lindsay McKinnon of Theatre of the Mind Productions. Available on Audible iTunes and Amazon. Follow Lindsay on Twitter at @Lindzmckinnon. Website TheatreOfTheMindProductions.com.

(I have been so lucky to meet Lindsay McKinnon – her narration has added a whole new dimension to the Curmudgeon Avenue Series)

Bronte Crescent, Radcliffe is fictional. There is a Bronte Avenue in Bury, just down the road. My husband lived here when I met him... how romantic!

I previously worked for the NHS, here I learnt that public sector offices move about for the fun of it, such as housing and social services in the same building. I had to give up my nursing career because I have Multiple Sclerosis.

To keep in touch with me, visit/follow my blog samanthahenthornfindstherightwords.blog Updates about Curmudgeon Avenue (and details of further books) will be published here.

I am also available on my Facebook page Samantha Henthorn. Author and Twitter @SamanthaHfinds.

Happy reading, Samantha.

THE FIRST CHAPTER OF THE HAROLD AND EDITH ADVENTURES (CURMUDGEON AVENUE BOOK TWO)

Chapter 1: Harold and Edith.

Manchester worker bees danced around the front gardens of Curmudgeon Avenue, in celebration of our return and anticipation of Harold and Edith's romantic adventure.

When we left them, Harold was all feet-under-the-table. Edith was having another one of her birthdays, and Edna had ruined it by announcing she was (allegedly) moving to France. Ricky Ricketts continued his on/off entanglement with Wantha, and there is a mystery involving Toonan. They are still a set of nincompoops, and I am *still* exasperated by their presence here. All you need to know (for now) is that Edna and Genevieve were travelling far away from Curmudgeon Avenue, albeit in the opposite direction of the Channel Tunnel. You see, if they did go to France, then someone – (Harold and Edith) would know where they were, should someone else (the French police) come looking for them and when I say them, I mean Genevieve.

'But why, Northumberland?' Edna protested on the Northeast bound road.

'The quiet, mon amie. No one will bother us there' Genevieve Dubois had always known how to push Edna's buttons.

'No one will bother us? Oh, how delightful!' How inconspicuous! I agree, Genevieve!'

'D'accord, Edna, D'accord' Said Genevieve.
And that was the last we heard of Edna, for now, that is...

Meanwhile, back at Curmudgeon Avenue, Harold was doing alright for himself. Who would have thought that after his rooftop protest in Radcliffe and his stint in the Salvation Army hostel he would end up being a fully paid-up member of Curmudgeon Avenue? (Albeit courtesy of the benefits agency). The luxury roof had been fitted, the insurance money had come through after the Georgina Foote incident, and Ricky Ricketts had moved back in with his on/off devotee Wantha. Ricky still had all his post delivered to Curmudgeon Avenue, I expect he had his reasons. And what about Edith? Oh yes, she was round the back, putting the bins out - you would think that Harold would do that for her, wouldn't you? But Harold was busy with his day time duties. Daily routine was important, especially for Harold. Paperwork to the benefits agency could take up a whole morning sometimes. And he had enough clothes to fill two tallboy chests of drawers, so choosing a T-shirt and getting dressed took its time. On her return from bin duty, Edith watched Harold preen himself in front of the mirror, making sure he had the correct clothing combination, so as not to reveal his flabby stomach. His jeans were ironed with a crease down the front. '*Who's that good looking chap?*' He would say to himself. Harold then told Edith she had 'Half an hour to get ready' and proceeded to spend twenty-five of those minutes in the bathroom making a smell and leaving Edith only five minutes to get ready.

Eventually, Harold and Edith went up Bury to the 'World Famous Market'. Parking OLD 50DG (Edith's car) on double yellow lines.

'Everyone's disabled in Bury these days Edith, the traffic warden won't notice us'. They had forgotten that the market is only open on Wednesday, Friday and Saturday. This was Tuesday, so they had to make do with the indoor fish and sundries stalls. 'Have you got any cash, Edith?' Harold said, in his *'I've got an idea'* voice. She handed over a ten-pound note. Harold treated Edith to some sarsaparilla tablets from *'Mrs Tuppence's Sweetie Stall'*. He pocketed Edith's change, and of course, Harold had the first one. Then he made that stupid joke; clamping his hand around the outside of the bag, holding the sweets in a vice-like grip, while at the same time pretending to offer Edith one by showing her the open bag.

'What's wrong, Edith? Can't you get one? Hehehe' as Harold laughed at Edith, a loud cracking sound could be heard. He dropped the bag of sweets and grabbed the side of his face. 'OWWWWWW ME BLOODY TOOTH'

'Oh, Harold!' cried Edith.

'First things first, Edith' still clutching the side of his face, drool pouring out of his mouth, Harold marched back to the sweet stall.

'I've seen that advert on telly' Harold started at the woman 'My tooth has been involved in an accident, and it was your entire fault' Harold wiped his disgusting drooling chin with the back of his jacket sleeve. 'I'll see you in court!' Harold said without explaining to Mrs Tuppence what on earth he was on about.

'I'll deny everything!' Mrs Tuppence gasped.

Litigation had become popular thanks to those TV adverts and despite most people's insistence that they '*Don't watch adverts*' everyone knows that *'Where there's blame, there's a claim!'* And so Mrs Tuppence and her sundries stall proprietors had all been on a course designed to fend off the likes of Harold. Edith was now on her hands and knees picking up the bag of sweets that Harold had dropped. You would think that Harold would help her, it's like the bin incident all over again... Mrs Tuppence was now on the customer side of her stall, firmly flicking the bird at the wounded Harold and the flummoxed Edith.

'Time to go home, Edith.' Harold said. By the time they returned to Curmudgeon Avenue, Edith had accumulated a parking ticket, and Harold's T-shirt was covered in saliva.

'You can 'phone the council over that ticket, if it's your first offence they will let you off' Harold asserted. This theory was neither true, nor was it Edith's first offence. Remember the Casanova incident? At least Maurice had saved Edith from a lost parking ticket, that one was her son's fault. This one was HAROLD'S FAULT. But Edith still loved him. Yes, that's what I said, LOVE, a word that has not been uttered in Curmudgeon Avenue for quite some time... Stuff was getting serious for Edith.

It turned out that a replacement filling was all that was required after the sarsaparilla tablet incident; however, Harold managed to claim a further five hundred pounds for loss of earnings. It only took a few weeks to put a claim in. Harold had been stalking the postman, eager for news about himself. Harold had even timed the poor postman, and awaited his delivery every single day. On this particular Monday, a letter arrived announcing itself with the plopping sound of post on the doormat and the clanking sound of a metal letterbox. Harold bounded down the stairs two steps at a time.

Brown envelopes addressed to Edith, 'No they must be bills' Harold said out loud, chucking the letters behind him '*Reader's Digest*, nope. *Thompson Local* 'Harold looked behind him eyeing Ricky Ricketts, trespassing in the kitchen, he shoved the telephone directory under his arm, it might come in handy.

'Anything for me?' asked Ricky.

'No... But here it is! Mr H Goatshed' Harold ripped open the letter from the litigation company. There it was his cheque for five hundred pounds! He read the letter out while gloating, of course.

Ricky looked bewildered. 'Loss of earnings?! You haven't even got a job!'

'I know!' Harold grinned 'But I could have. They don't know that!' Ricky Ricketts did not know whether to admire Harold or belittle him, and so he said:

'Nice one Harold, you jammy git.'

Harold was so pleased with his result that he could not stop. Blaming, claiming and complaining became his full-time job/hobby. He wrote all kinds of letters and filled in numerous forms. To the council for the exposed manhole, he tripped over. To the water board for the hole in the pavement he threw himself down, and everyone's favourite, green crisps! Harold received a year's supply of free replacement crisps posted to Curmudgeon Avenue. Custard creams with no cream in, jam doughnuts with no jam in. A bunch of flowers bought for Edith that surprisingly enough, did not keep her happy for the guaranteed seven days - Harold complained. He even sussed out how to take all the toothpaste out of a tube while making it look like a new one, but hollow inside. This resulted in several refunds from several chemists. Money back guarantees and self-inflicted injuries were no obstacle to Harold.

Then there was the local kebab shop and its slippery floor that Harold pretended to slip and fall on. This is where Harold's cashing in story ends. Who would have thought that his fellow customer that day would be Psycho Steve? (Remember him from the Bridge Tavern in Radcliffe?). Popping chip after greasy chip in his mouth, he observed Harold back and forth trying to skate across the tiled floor, until he purposely crashed like a baby giraffe into the corner.

'Help! Help!' Harold had this practised rigmarole to perfection 'I've obviously broken my meta-tarsal!' Harold mistakenly clutched his left shin.

'I wish I had caught that on camera!' Psycho Steve laughed, spitting sodden grease potato everywhere 'Two hundred and fifty quid if you send that sort of thing into the telly!'

Harold expertly opened his right eye and whispered 'Wanna go halves?' to Psycho Steve, who huffed and shook his head in mock disbelief.

'No charge, Steve' the kebab shop owner returned from the back of the shop, shaking hands with Psycho Steve. Why does HE have to have so many friends?! Soon, the kebab shop owner was filled in as to what had happened, not by Harold (who remained clutching his shin on the floor) but by Psycho Steve, (Sleeveless Steve arrived now, and joined in the conversation about how dodgy Harold is.) It turned out that Harold's performance was captured on CCTV, the kebab shop owner had been on the same course that Mrs Tuppence from Bury Market had. Cameras were installed to deflect responsibility for any slippery floor shenanigans. The kebab shop owner momentarily turned the CCTV off so that he could 'have a word' with Harold, thus ending his complaining money making scheme. Harold did not want to talk about it, not to Edith, or to anyone.

MORE BY THE AUTHOR.

The Harold and Edith Adventures (Curmudgeon Avenue Book Two)

When we return to Curmudgeon Avenue in book two, Harold and Edith embark on their romantic adventure, Ricky Ricketts continues his on/off entanglement with Wantha Rose, Edna is missing presumed living in France, and the house itself is still exasperated - but wait! Who is this mysterious man driving his expensive car up and down Curmudgeon Avenue? For readers who enjoy the delightful Manchester sense of humour, this book will make you smile.

https://www.amazon.co.uk/dp/B07J2P5PZS
https://www.amazon.com/dp/B07J2P5PZS

Edna and Genevieve Escape From Curmudgeon Avenue (Book Three)

When Genevieve Dubois returned to Curmudgeon Avenue, this opened up the opportunity for Edna to realise her long-held dream of escaping to France. But as Edna embraces all things European, Genevieve appears to be shying away from her French roots.

Meanwhile, returning to Curmudgeon Avenue for the third time, the wind had blown in the truth about the tall, handsome stranger and although Harold and Edith had been relieved to discover that he is neither an elephant detective, nor a fraud investigator, Toonan had been a little disappointed that he was not interested in her

either. Matteo Dubois was looking for his mother, Genevieve Dubois, and although he did not find her on Curmudgeon Avenue, you have probably guessed that he is about to cause a disturbance-FINALLY! There is hope that the set of nincompoops that live here currently will move out and leave me in peace! Edna had already escaped with Genevieve to France, which was a real shame for me because Edna was one of the less annoying ones. This delightful third off-beat comedy romance book in the Curmudgeon Avenue series will make you smile
https://www.amazon.com/dp/B07N2YCXV5
https://www.amazon.co.uk/dp/B07N2YCXV5

The Ghosts of Curmudgeon Avenue (Book Four)

The house on Curmudgeon Avenue should be happy now, the nincompoop residents have all met their sorry ends. But they haven't quite left... now that a new family move in can the house find peace? Or are the ghosts of Curmudgeon Avenue going to interfere with the goings-on, romance and dramas that new residents bring?

Gordon and Zandra Bennett - along with their lovelorn daughter Krystina move all the way from London to Curmudgeon Avenue. Zandra has her heart set on renovating the four-storey Victorian terrace and hires Harry to rip out the old and bring in the new. Wonder how that will go down with the grumpy, yet proud house? Not to mention Harold, Edna and Edith who are trapped in their previous home with no choice but to haunt Krystina, moan about the renovations and get up to mischief.

https://www.amazon.co.uk/dp/B07YN8SBBK
https://www.amazon.com/dp/B07YN8SBBK

1962.

Ernest Bradshaw has grit and determination, but best of all, Ernest Bradshaw has ambition, the ambition to become the next cycling champion to hail from 1960's Lancashire. Problem is, the threat of nuclear war is looming - and his mother is petrified. If you like a good, nostalgic story, you need to read '1962' and join Ernest and the wonderful array of characters' journey into life, love, and the ups and downs of cycling with a backdrop of global uncertainty.
https://www.amazon.co.uk/dp/B074P5TNTJ
https://www.amazon.com/dp/B074P5TNTJ

Piccalilly. : A Remembrance Day Story.

Piccalilly is a short novel about Lillian, an eight-year-old girl who is missing her older brother, Joe. He has been serving in the army in World War One. When Lillian's parents receive a telegram informing them of the worst, Lillian discovers that Joe's spirit is living on in a series of comforting events.
Piccalilly is based around a true story, in memory of the author's family. Written originally for the author's mother.
https://www.amazon.co.uk/dp/B01MAYULK1
https://www.amazon.com/dp/B01MAYULK1

Quirky Tales to Make Your Day.

Aliens on the beach in Brighton, a washing machine's memoirs, a couple who do not like their new neighbours, missing underwear, a witch hunt, Kurt Cobain's ghost, two crimes, revenge and many more. All these stories look at the quirky side of life and will instantly make your day because if you like the title, you'll love a good story.

https://www.amazon.co.uk/dp/B06XT7TJ6Y
https://www.amazon.com/dp/B06XT7TJ6Y

Printed in Great Britain
by Amazon